The Palm Reading after The Toad's Garden

The Palm Reading after The Toad's Garden

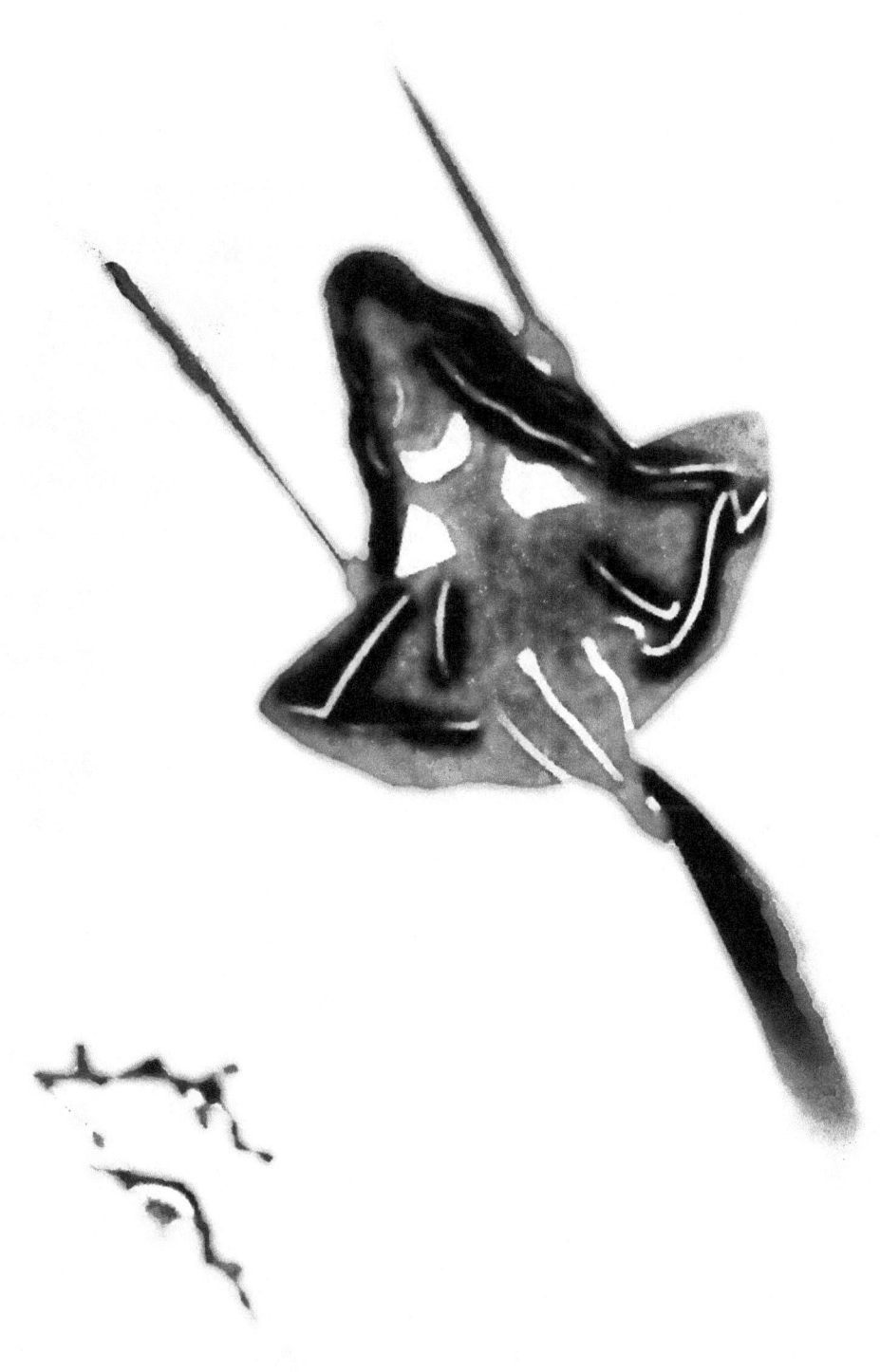

The Palm Reading after The Toad's Garden

Michael Dickel

Is A Rose Press

2016

Hybrid
Flash Fiction
Poetry
Short Stories

Cover and book design: Jacob Palm

is a rose press publishes poetry, experimental writing, hybrid and other work. We are a cooperative editorial board of writers in the virtual world. Submissions are by invitation only at this time. Check our website for updates and changes in this policy.

Website: isarosepress.WordPress.com

Dickel, Michael (b. 1955)
The Palm Reading after The Toad's Garden

   is a rose press

   1. Hybrid 2. Fiction; short stories. 3. Flash Fiction. 4. Poetry. 5. Cross-genre. 6. Experimental writing.

   I. Title: The Palm Reading after The Toad's Garden.

is a rose press
minneapolis-missoula

ISBN   978-0-9896245-4-1

for Aviva

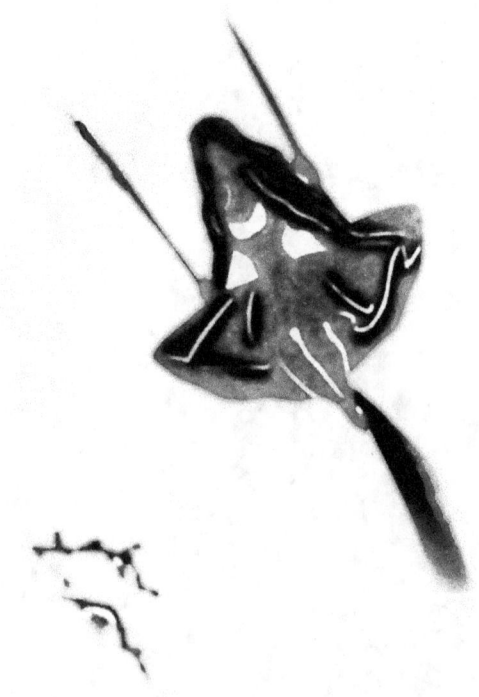

The Palm Reading after
The Toad's Garden

The Toad's Garden

The Palm Reading

The Toad's Garden

The Toad's Garden

The Woman with a Beard
(Chicken and Egg)

Tomorrow

The lump of garbage will linger below the shallow winds before a whisper, a snicker really, can startle ears into flight. The bearded woman takes off her jacket that fateful night, her slender rear a blip in the unnamed prattle that will surge over the gully. Her foot will ride out of the sneaker as she recalls her smooth-faced lover.

Not much of the dark remains. The coming day crosses the paths of people, lingers below consciousness as pale light shimmies out of its nightgown. Her lover left a note, C-sharp, echoing on the piano. It grates onions over the volley, rounds blasting from cannon on the cliffs. Silhouettes slide across the sea's horizon, warships invading again.

The fight had been brief. Her smooth-faced lover wanted her beard, not her heart. He cursed his Anishinabe rootlessness. Paper-airplane resumés boomeranged around them. Work. The mold rejected them, refused to grow even on their old oranges. Stars faded. The night wanted to escape.

The sneaker slips to the floor, a thump against sleep. Fighting the tide of dreams, she prepares to slip out, under cover of the winds. Now naked. Alone. She crosses the gully, mounts the hill, lights the bonfire. The road to town mocks her. Standing on the cliff she waits. Smooth faces attract her. Her naked skin drinks single malt whiskey while making up stories for invisible companions.

"Good-bye," the piano note hums.
"I can't live here anymore."

The smoke stench coats her. A poor blanket, but who knew then. She looks out at the frigates shrinking out of perspective.

Then she goes to bed.

§

Today

Boots glitter down rain-drenched paths, sheep trails really. Clouds scream past jets standing at attention over the melted-glass sea. The woman with the beard met her smooth-faced lover at a bar over the hills and past two towns. Refracted drops of rain drip off the grasses. Tired flights of birds shiver trees, as the drowsy film skips its sprockets in the middle of the romantic scene.

She mounts the cliffs. His galleon sailed, sank, salted away in a bank account she has no number or password for. The water whines, dark red shadows swirling. He bought her whiskey, smoked her hair with cigarettes. Carried off by nomads. The beating drums. Her mind mixed into music rocking down the stoney way.

What washing machines cook on the
gas range, casts iron out of the pans.
Emergent molecules develop atomic movies,
entertaining faster than the light particles
with popcorn imitations. Mystics could
not imagine the empty vessels of cyborg
social-network terror cells recombining
synthetic DNA along the runway. It's
another dream, "a Box of Rain" sung to
the strum of guitars. She missed the turn
at the car speedway, Mother's Day 1973,
Des Moines, Iowa, and spun out into orbit
around glimmering promises. Before.

The photographer jacketed the digital
sleeve surrounding still moments.
Necrophilia began with literature then
moved on to still cameras, expanded
with movies and talkies and quickies.
Entropy sways the glyphs along silver
screens, our lives screened by so
many lookers gazing at nothing.

So she took the smooth-faced lover home. Why not? And it wasn't so bad, not really. Warm bears in bed, unstuffed and compliant to desires not his or her own. Winter hibernation arrives without warning. The coals burn low; by itself, an ember goes out. Spring cubs run around the melting snow. That was all so long ago.

He doesn't stand under the waterfalls. Trees paint shadows. She sang sad songs by the shore in a minor. Key. He countered with his note on the piano—C#. Falling into sevenths, an odd fraction to uncover a piece of the pie.

Despite everything, she goes off to work.

§

Morning

She enjoyed his propensity for Joycean
density. Lingual logistics, caliper calisthenics
precisely measuring misfired exercises
of desire. Inventive ventures vanished,
evaporated under the heat of disillusionment
dissolving distances. Modern nomads
surfing channels, bounced from screen
to network to social interchange, a spider
caught in the web. A fly uncomfortable
company. Nomadic exchange rates duly
noted and time differences computed.

Unruly arithmetic. Time-and-a-half.
Double-time, he marched double-time,
the smooth-faced lover, into and then out
of two-timing three-timing four-timing.
A dollar store. She saw them in the dollar
store. Where he worked. They worked.

Flagrant fellatio delecto in fragrant modes,
blossoms scented sensuously around the
room. Candles glassed in, clever collisions of
molecules escaping into light. Enter the light.

She thinks morning the best time to die.
Death doesn't knock on the door. It rings
a silent bell. *Beneath the waves, under the
cliff,* she thinks. *That is where death drifts.*

Beleaguered at her job, her boss
demanding she shave reality to corner the
market on advertising. Social media, search
engine optimization, fine-tuned to deliver.
Buyers, like sea gulls, follow the fishing
boat hoping for scraps of nourishment.
The nets closed around her hair when she
worked fast food. Let her write right rites
of persuasion and pie filling that sounds
like cherry bombs dusted to crazy.

Who uncovers the bearded woman's
favorite jacket fetish, uncovers her secret
shoes, uncovers her naked skin telling
made up stories about its colorful past
while drinking whiskey, single malt, belly
to the bar. He who uncovers these uncovers
her hair. Her smooth-faced lover knew.
He could smell his own lies on her breath.
She resonated like a tocsin bell. While
wringing her hands around her empty chest
cracked open imprecisely, the momentum
carries him in. He drank in her. Habits
grow, flower, fruit. Her wine matured.

In 1972 she should have run off with the boy who had the long, golden hair. His leather jacket hung better than any man's fantasy. The grass under him stayed dry. The evening summer sun sunk, cinders sparked from a campfire someone lit. Ripple spread out, around, bottle unscrewed. Nomads searching for the right guitar chord—F, a bar chord, hard on the fingers.

Her fingers on his hardness. Yet she did not stick out her thumb as he hitched a ride come morning. She saw him roll his sleeping bag. Gather his pack. Walk away from the cold, charred scar at the center. She could picture the rest, the highway, the upheld thumb, the car pulling over.

She surfs now all the channels and webs, but he eludes her. Perhaps he never bought a TV, doesn't have computer or cable.

§

Afternoon

Rain falls into the morning, fizzles as
clouds disperse and heat glares out at the
world. Afternoon sun follows channels,
another flash flood eroding the side of a
wadi. Past its zenith, gold fades. Too many
additives alloyed to gravity pull poised carats
out. She watches the dry, hot day blanch
as though it would faint. The ring of light
plays through her irises, turns those eyes,
once tiger bright, into broken agates.

So, the woman with a beard thinks, 1969
ended it all. Music faded. Smoke rose up
and drifted away. Traveling lovers left no
memories but a sort of longing that leaned
up against the door and looked through
slit eyes. Ah, that one had a black pony
tail pulled back tight around his head, a
death skull skirting skirmishes, sulking
sidelong glances, startling glazed-doe
eyes. Hendrix kissed good-bye, played
jazz riffs while laying on the bed, idly.
Perhaps something familiar passed notes
this way, the key. G. Light burning out.

The smooth-faced lover lost most
recently danced. Bars bounced outside
his body, it seemed, his movements so
collected contained all movements to the
point of still. Her eyes glued to his fluid
interpretations of the world, she missed
the tug that took her in, off balance, to this
gravitational field. Magnetic charm cheated
words, left her breathless, motionless, lost.

She loses the train, tracks melting in the
heat, of thought. Her boss presses forward
in straight lines of commodification,
codification, commerce, copulation
replacement communication, closing
the sale, consummation, consumption.
Repeat. From here to there and there to
somewhere else. Hard on logic, soft on
value, all contented encapsulation of
energy, power, money—conservation of
energy, momentum, synergy, entropy—
hammered into an out-of-the-box lack of
creation that boxes frying pan and fire into
tiny wavelets of frozen food convenience.

She longs to slip out of this job, her
clothes, her skin, to touch possibilities,
connections, resonances, vibrating through
her, pulsating into her—trust. Touch. Know.

After work, the
sea calls, the beach
cries out in a lover's
response. Beach-bar
crowd, single-malt
pacification, calming
of the invasion. The
aliens, indeed, came
in business suits.
Warships hover just
over the horizon, lost
from sight but always
present, the sense of
them, the shadows
projected up through
an orange globe sun.
Worshippers come
drumming and dancing
to see it fall, this red-
shifting star, into the
sea. No steam rises.

She watches dancers.
They let the room
define them, do not
defy the music, deify
the steps. She sips, slips
into reverie revolving
around revolutions
that fell apart. Jobs
shrunk back, everyone
panicked, and the
masters of corporate
feudalism again
controlled the serfs.
As the surf calms for
sunset, she relaxes.
What else to do?

The sellers marketed
everything they could, pushed
away everything they could
not, attacked what threatened
to return. They scared us all
into convincing them we were
unworthy of their miserly support
but would give them everything
for this chance at livelihood.
Tom Sawyers with their gold
fences painted white. Like rich
relatives who don't want to
acknowledge you, they allowed
us to serve them, she thinks,
according to their will and whim.

The bonfires went
unattended, mostly. The
revolutionary sparks spread too
thin. She sips her whiskey.

The sun sets.

§

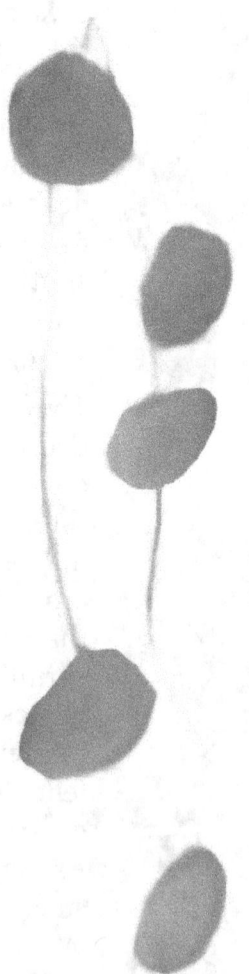

Evening

Time slows as light escapes and shadowed
night falls over her face. Waves glitter
moonlit sonatas in soporific rhythms
of heart beat, lost sleep, then run deep
in memory. Wet sand shines. The malt
whiskey-mellow mood soaks into wind
whispering patterns of hush, hush, hush.
The bearded woman wishes for her nomadic
life, no one's wife wishes as fervently.

Neutralized like lost neutrinos whose
loose cable sped them beyond light, she
floats in her beach bar chair, feet digging dry,
warm sand. Dinner din rises, falls, rises, falls
from inside and outside, all around her the
social groupings of ritual meeting, eating,
drinking, mating. This world whirls faster
through space than she can comprehend.
Physics unravels the surrounding universes.

Night fall, an illusion. It rises up in
the shadow of the earth around them.
Out beyond shadow or illusion, light
remains. Moon reflects evidence, an
occasional passing satellite agrees, the
spots of planets, if she could recall which
and where, concur. Time measures itself
in movement through space while flying
particles imagine themselves still. Like her
smooth-faced lover who so engaged dance
that he seemed still, the world flowing
around him impossibly in motion.

He did move. Into her life. Into her
house. And, now, out of it. Gone. Like
the hitchhiker long ago, and the man
with the long ponytail before him.

Like 1967, the Summer of Love finished
and gone. She stood on a street in the
Haight one day, watching people. Then she
went to Golden Gate Park for the funeral.
Men, or probably boys from her current
perspective, waved top hats, wore odd
clothes from other eras, bright clothes tie-
dyed last week. Women, or likely girls like
her, showed scads of skin, tie-dye coverings,
with vintage wear mixed and matched, furs
even. Everyone strung out with beads. Dress-
up days. Long flowing hair. Afros. The coffin
hand-painted, a sign on the side: Summer
of Love. Behind it, the corpse of Hippie.
The Diggers dug it down to the grounded
burial plot, tried to bury it next to money.

Hippie had died, they said. Killed by the
media. Overexposed and misrepresented.
Time covered the funeral, photo-spread
opportunity. Maybe the counter culture
period began here, or perhaps freaks
freighted feverish transition into then.

Escapades of escaped expression
extended from happenings into mediated
madness; Hollywood and Madison Avenue
caught the wave and surfed into the scene
with conspicuous desire for consumption.
She watched the mock funeral laugh at
itself and joined in; Julia Vinograd blew
bubbles in the procession. Someone said
Ginsberg had come, but not that she saw.

A boy on stilts walked in the funeral, from the funeral into her life. She circled him on the street, he bent down, handed her a joint. Smoke and mirrors present, multimedia wonderment, diamond dream reflection, ghost stories and revelations. Rainbows refracted from his prism glasses. Nothing near but naked skin and slippery sweat.

They swam at Muir Beach. They meandered or stumbled through fairytale-fogged redwoods. One day, he drifted into the riptide and floated down to LA. She climbed a tree and joined a commune. Rumors reached out to her, reveling in revelations that he followed the Dead around the world, stilt walking the crowds and selling on the side.

Beach bar community buzzes, bees making honey. She follows the flower trail out of the whiskey haze and picks her path home. The gully crossed, she winds her way under the wind, tight into the pattern now, checkerboard laid bare, check and mate.

Matter never quite coalesced from the rambling energy randomly dominating her. She makes her way into the place, a sort of shelter sorting her out near the beach but away from everything, equidistant from the sun.

Shaking dinner from the kitchen, she eats what she wants and no more. Perhaps that is the pattern, she reflects. Then she swims into sleep on the sofa.

§

Yesterday

Waking wired, wound 'round spools
spinning space and time into brief episodic
memories, dream-drips not quite joining
into a garden reflecting pool, a toad's
gardenia mirror. The woman with a beard
rises warily, sensing her smooth-faced
lover's scent; a single-point singularity draws
every line to its perspective; all thoughts
crush under their own weight, absolute
zero, frozen atoms collapsing around her.

Asteroids drift across galaxies. Emotional
vampires—vapid, pale—float above every
wound. Still seized by decades flown
past a million miles of space journey or
more ago, she shakes graying hair loose
from sleep, finger-combing combustible
comprehension into something smooth.

Way down below the ocean, down deep
under the sea, death drifts. The shadow of
warships do not reach its lair. She reaches
out her mermaid hands to feel the bone
rubbed smooth by all who have drunk
the brine. Once she flew high and wide,
wildly searching, quests without questions,
travel without destination. Now she sinks
or swims, deep into or out of dream.

On the commune she worked the vegetables, hand-hoeing weeds, topless in the turbid heat caressing her. They played Frisbee totally naked in the grass, slowing sluggish traffic on the county road, attracting road workers who ate their lunch as close as they dared, while commune members danced in dizzy drizzle from sprinkler heads. Honeybees buzzed the air around flowers and forested hills, their boxed supers out back.

Before the harvest, the others drifted into bars, back to cities, out of the community. Her then lover, who called herself the mad painter, took off with the dumpy man who brought eggs every morning. His wife wept tears of joy to be free of his philandering pheromones. The woman with the beard bought chickens from her, raised a rickety henhouse, and no longer needed egg deliveries, although longing.

She stretches up into this morning, mourning
all past particles as she touches the smooth-
faced lover still asleep, wanting him up and out
of her bed. His groans grumble, resonant entropy
waking to momentum. His will does not wake.

Tomorrow. Or the next day. He will write a note. Off-
key. He will leave it on the piano. He will leave.

See how sharp the resonant echoes play. Jazz dissonance.

Breaking fast or slow, eating now or later, piecing it
all together, her real eyes contracting into realization:
she wants him to go. She has been waiting.

She thinks about buying some hens.

§

The Toad's Garden

Reflections on the Toad's Garden
(Deciduous Mirror Reflecting)

Butterfly Effect: Chaos on a Shoe String

Butterfly on a shoe—a constant bliss, elated and surreal, some automatic writing made from fresh warm milk—dreams of rain. The desert sunset signifies peace to the gopher writing its manifesto far from the Saskatchewan railroad's violence. A nasty sherbet left a taste of forgotten hypocrisy like a flashbulb memory in his mouth, burnt like boiled-over soup on the stove top. The moon mirrors his face, its shadow-craters another dimension.

Greed spills blood through the nun's hands, nuclear waste pouring out her fingers. What bread will she eat, this stench of death in her nose? Lady Macbeth knew blood and hands and death. The ocean breeze ruffles her hair like forest leaves, while the sea's salt walks the dog like sweet coffee travels through the night, Mercury retrograde, with nomadic drivers hustling the highway for spare change at the pool table before dawn.

The tulip knows cold winds, playing Scrabble, drinking mint tea under the snow, waiting for the cardinal's lonely, red, winter vigil to leap up into spring. The spirit needs rest. Karma suffers bouts of cold and sweat; hot, dull space drips its indigo cello-blue into Luce Iragary's recursive folding of flesh away from and toward the center, touching Cixous' brushing, together, moments of possibility.

The cat in the sky sits on the green roof, thinks, "time to go."

The Other Day

The woman with a beard insists on
returning time and again to the past,
resurrected on a credit card. Clouds, pink,
grey, tinge morning's eastern flowers,
trees silhouetted with birds singing. The
day's chaperone opens the door and she
strolls down to the creek. The screen
slams shut while the computer cursor
floats over the images, seeks links.

Never, she thinks. Never can she recall
anytime worse or better. Yet each recollection
collates her emotions into collections of
missed chances, chance misses, all chance
encounters, no path or purpose. My
church window—most likely, glass from
a bottle on an anvil—would branch paths
predicated on doing nothing; I'm not an
expert, she thinks. An expert and a green
sweater would be just right in each case.

The polar night of memory courses
along protons and electrons, north
and south magnetic fields shaping
the almond flower in soft moonlight.
Stranded dresses turn up in the rock
tumbler, polished like sheets of mica.

Sunrise, though, its scarlet monopoly
on the world, takes backseat to no
melody. Floating on the wings of maybe,
the woman with the beard stretches
arms toward the new day. Gamma floats
between alpha and omega, gimmel a game
between aleph and tav. A single ray of
sun hits the creek from under the blood-
colored cloud of mourning nostalgia, false
memory, flashing like bits of dream.

Love is the law now, physics mixed with
mysticism and life a passing energy come
to wake matter, stir it to potential beyond
physicality. Memory dissipates, evaporates
as the fog of dawn clears from her waking
mind, a trinket that would traffic in
trigonometry across a toad's forest plaza.

§

The Toad's Garden

A trinket from space that will traffic in trigonometry falls across the toad's forest plaza. Love, without sex, creates a constant in the calculations of nothing. The toad lives on a nice and norval diggery ave, where it wonders, *Where's my gawddamn slippers gorn?!?!*

It's all a straw dog drawn along the floor. The capacitor follows the missing lines of calculations to enter an elephant. Mercury in retrograde or quicksilver at your feet, tosh. The grumpy steel worries when it will fall, effervescent sparks pluming, lonely, into the rolling molds.

The woman with the beard feels fright for the toad, poor wretch, while tending her garden. The rain-pulse pounds down the crimson flowers. Their efflorescence is the pneuma she seeks to savor. *It is a stretch to deliver this thought to her tongue, precocious and fleeting this, and you, yet, still want it,* she thinks. Her tongue tastes salty sweat trickling in the heat.

Reflexive Properties

Another bit of this and that from the
net of ether, screened reality through
spidered-network sociability unfolding
in cyberspace-time. So much folderol,
foolish nonsense on shiny screens an
anesthetic pigsty, un-aesthetic style pick.
The old don't mollycoddle around with
quotidian living—a day is not just a day
when nearing the end of closing networks,
out-of-work servers laying down their
hard-driving rain. Unemployment controls.
The sentence unfolds. The comma at the
end causes trauma. *Pissed, one day us
guys went up to the Five, 2+3, 3+2, reflexive
properties*, the drunk man mutters, sinks
into his misting beer at the bar below
as the woman with a beard watches.

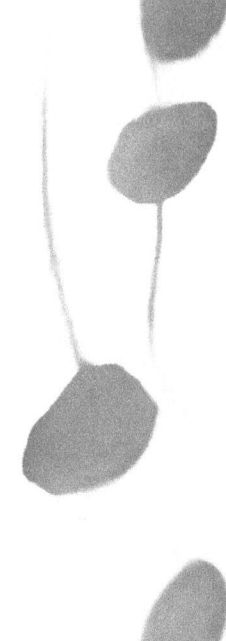

The beach cafe. So many bars, so many
drowning folk stories, blew sung winds. The
cook would fry up some creepers, tender.
Drinking from this bitter gourd leaves a taste
unwanted but accepted by sad nostalgic
nasturtiums nested next to the path.

She wants to understand, to hold
hope and have. Musty memories mold
and deny understanding—possessing
geometric properties, recursive; hurt
hops off hope, spins it out of control over
a cliff. Crash and burn in the sunshine
of you are my... *Sing this, if you can,* she
would say to the folk singer at one end
of space, but that singer would not listen
from her end of time. A child, really.

*A taste of salt this work, letters blowing
away in sand,* she sings to herself, these
songs that do not end but echo endless
mnemonic caverns, turn on the wing
of a tern or sea gull over the beach, as
she sips slowly her whiskey whispers.

It's a promise, a creed, torch burning, the
physiognomy of tomorrow that can mortify
yesterday following an estuary as the gull
turns. *This bird teaches a Socratic method
without refrain,* she thinks. *A wonder-wench
would dream it diving, deliberately darting,
daring.* The gull shrieks off in a pussyvan.

Palatalized consonants
by palatines speak любовь,
love, Lilith stealing away
the night, haunting
campfires of paleolithic
desires, hunting spheres
of influence emanating
distinctions heard by
Red Heifer herds.

Laughing women three
tables over wear different
vintage sunburnt skins,
slouching at the table
while watching each other,
murder the disposition of
their eyes, as they recall
betrayals, stolen lovers,
sunshine my you are and
traffic heavy, heaving
across causeways narrowly
traversed. Their radio
blasted beach-combers
who did not listen or hear
here, near the heart, while
hair twisted blue fingers.
The lineup stretches
into grief, solitary and
communal. Later, over
coffee, they will mention
Montreal, a golf ball,
and how much someone
worries while on the run.

§

Word-tossed Salad

The woman with a beard strolls to the station through sunshine cutting like a blade. A duck swims in the pond to resonate resoundingly with restructured memories of chickens. A Brobdingnagian sense of largeness, largess from the Cajun Country music—Zydeco rides a coat of paint, counts rhythmically sensational sensual expansion on her timpani membrane.

A dingleberry drops on the earwig, unerringly resting in the shade of the toad's garden beneath a diachrony in space, the way her smooth-faced lover two-timed her tune, thyme in the chicken, parsley in the salad, sage advice, rosemary babying bye and bye. The real bird next to a cement-statue bird counts to five, standing still to still stand after the hunter.

Wharves sing to the waves, sea goings-on and off the sand, as autumn cascades corpulently toward the Bogpan peninsula. It all lowers and raises the living, shimmering question, *what if?* in her shimmed mind, off-balance scales, that way nothing.

To understand hope, to deny hurt, to sing. Elaboration is a form of pollution, her mind skips to my Lou. Walk walk green green skip my jolly flowering grasses. Cobalt blue sky calms clammy fear of the afternoon moon but nowhere recalls verbatim, an exceptional, lowly ingrate of an orang-utan twisting, elastic. Word salad tossed to the breeze, un-solid world twisting in solid up-borne whirligig wind, elephantine ego elastically sutured to the.

§

Deciduous Mirror Reflecting

The woman with a beard kneels to readjust
the Lilliputian fulcrum of the toad's garden,
reading between the lines of papyrus to the
tune of an amphibious plop. The succinct,
princely frog reflects in the deciduous mirror
as it drops its leaves in a stellar reflection
of night. Toad's green cousin in full glory.

In 1968, the world revolted. *Revolutionary
fires return to this garden night*, she reflects.
Arterial blood flows through starlight as a
feather drops and the ripples encompass
the earth in chaotically flapping butterfly
wings. Egypt. Turkey. Greece. Japan.

The clematis bloom glows, a heavenly
reminder of possibility in the face of
probability, the white of snow turning blue.
Time lights a candle in the spire of the flower
as it writes caviardage: Be vast, matter, aye ye
windmill, eye the coming winds of change.
The garden waits. Time decides the status of
weed or flower; hybrid history names epochs.

She robes herself against nakedness, the woman with a beard, standing there in the weather. Silk spreads softly, bringing with it its own fan of hyperbole. She smells the fecundity of toad, frog, garden, prince. Not aspartame-fake sweet, but a hieroglyphic packed with ritualized sacrifice, she thinks:

Her smooth-faced lover, cut out of her heart. The mad painter she erased, the crumbs brushed away. The stilted lover drifted away, followed the Dead. The tall one with the laser eyes, a space oddity, glazed over, lost to her world. The boy with the golden hair, driven out, away.

She throws rice grown in fish pits into the pond in the toad's garden. The koi rise to the occasional flirting swallow twisting across a glimmering surface on a rolling basis, lapping pink from the sunset reflection. The toad thinks that pearls pester him, but not as much as they do the oyster.

She watches the water, then a tree girdled with carved lines from Gertrude Stein, sees a rose and thinks of the word love. What is it? A cheetah racing away or a crow cawing raucously to others? Not a stickler for such images, her property proves a gravitational magnet, her heart attracts ice, its melting memory a peripheral-vision flash as an icicle comes crashing down with a wallop.

Reflections on the Toad's Garden

The toad from the garden sent the woman with a beard a Valentine every year. As he usually hibernated at that time of year, he arranged it through an agency. It encouraged her to feed the garden and take care of him, his geometry, and the calculus of time as they unfolded in chaos theory across the tiny fulcrum at the center of tadpole pool, an island of insanity he installed one year, being a rather handy toad.

He did not scrimp in his work, seeking his goal to fuse time and space into a grand unified theory of dreamscapes spinning out from a spiral arm of a galaxy sailing through the universe at incredible but reducing velocity.

The woman with the beard realized that the toad did not send the Valentine and that his reasons for having it sent had more to do with utilitarianism than desire. Still, she tended the garden. Each spring, she planted the outline of a house with sunflower seeds and morning glories.

The morning glories climbed up the sturdy scaffolding of the sunflower stalks and created blooming walls by summer. Here she would set up lawn chairs and a table and spend many a summer afternoon with the toad, learning about how photons could entangle even before both of them existed, suggesting that entanglement perhaps tunneled through time, like certain encryption techniques using fiber optics.

Sometimes a tortoise joined them for iced tea and added his ponderous theories of inter-folded parallel universes that derived directly from possible world philosophy, only without the theology.

By fall, the birds came to raid the
sunflower seeds. In the winter, the
tall stalks with any remaining heads
served as bird feeders, too. Sometimes
bears stripped them bare.

And the following spring, the woman
with the beard started the cycle again
with a wave of her hands, as it were,
as she spread the next year's seed.

The toad approved. And she always
assisted with his garden. In this way, the
two of them lived in not-quite-symbiotic
relatedness, as close as, and a great deal more
honest than, most human couples ever get.

The toad only left for meditative higher
planes, never on a jet plane, and always
in the main remained right where she
could find him. And she never questioned
his mathematical improbabilities or the
raison-d'etre of the garden, or his French
accent. They simply settled into a habit,
side by side, and purposely left each
other to pursue their hirsute pursuits, her
beard, his chaos spun-string theories.

Thinking of this, she drifted back to the beach bar with her collection of Valentines in hand, sorting out a toad's love call from the occasional punctuations of human lovers come and gone.

The thing was, the math made sense, the addition and subtraction of others that ended up coming down to zero plus one. The theory had no holes in it that she could find. And memory won out each time she tried to look toward a future. Thus, possible worlds branched from past recollections, like these Valentine cards and the whiskey with the melting ice cubes swirling in her glass.

§

The Toad's Garden

A Visit
(Soon the Trumpets)

Dream Fishers

The woman with a beard dreams
constantly of death. Stone shadows stretch
to luminous horizons held at bay by
bestiaries embroidered into tapestries tap-
dancing tangents to King Carol's ballad
ballast. She would sink rather than throw
over the weightiness of such formative
songs sung blue, everybody knows that,
except the dream weaver whose catcher's
net fell onto the bed one sultry-sex night.
Whether death comes for her or her
mother, she could not say, but so far no
lover has died and her mother forgets her
way forward in the timeline left her.

Who would blame her this anxiety
balanced on a beam of the toad's leverage,
the fulcrum of the reflecting pool calculated
somehow using pi, imaginary numbers, and
theoretical physics? She wakes, shudders
off the spider webs of Thanatos and lights
the fires of libido, id, and ego. Bee supers
buzz around her head as she tries to avoid
the trap of dull songs numbing the inside
of her brain, stuck in frenzied repetition.

She lived among many lovers, each fallen
by the shore of the Fisher King. Galahad
never existed except in legend, and even
then only as a flawed reflection of ideal
gender expectations. So philosophies flower
in the hedgerows alongside the tawny rose
petals preserved in the summer heat.

The toad calls her to the garden and she would rather join him than linger in linguistic memories that try but fail to recover the essential oils of moments long gone. She steps into her cotton skin, drinks coffee cold-brewed.

When she goes outdoors, she finds blue sun and yellow sky splendor, a reversal of color a gift of imagery from the toad. Another day unfolds, and this day she chooses to let the sabbath arrest her, to drink wine and eat bread on the porch.

She thinks, *dear Saturday, let me rest with you.*

Thus she enters the court of the Fishers, trying to wake them from their somnolence. The land dries out, the people cry out, the blood flows out from the wounds of war.

Wake, Fishers, wake! She thinks. But they do not.

§

A Visit

Since forever
the toad had not
been an Anabaptist
abecedarian, but
a Zen Beginner's
Mind abecedarian or
perhaps an acrostic
puzzled down the
page. The toad
entered alphabetic
and other learning
from the start.

So he watched the
sunflower resin as
it dripped in a ratio
meant to glorify the
morning blossoms
until they shimmered
for *Iriya Asagao
Matsuri*. The thick
sticky substance
would bury itself
among the tangled
roots of sunflower
and morning glory,
thinning with the
soil's moisture to
the thickness of
molasses in summer.

This morning, while the toad
watched in his garden, the woman with
a beard made her way along store-lined
sidewalks past the barber, whose portrait
of Richard Nixon shaking his hand
faded in the front window, right by the
machine that ate plastic and excreted
cash, to number four on Main Street.

She entered the home as though
swimming upstream in the sand flowing
through an hourglass, pouring herself into
the rapidly expanding emptiness of lost time.
The nurse waiting inside greeted her with a
nod as she signed in at the front desk, and
then buzzed her through the locked door.

The woman with a beard continued
on her own down the hall. She always felt
her age and then some in this place, the
weight of her lifespan added to her mother's
coiled around her shoulders and draped
down her back, a heavy rope practicing
to transform itself into a python. About
three-quarters of the way down the hall,
she knocked lightly, then entered a room.

Inside, her mother sat in a swivel recliner
chair that, with the dresser along the wall,
represented a life-time of furniture that
once crowded the family's house. Her
mother stared out the window, as she did
every day, according to what the woman
with the beard learned from the staff.

Certainly, she sat there staring every Sunday morning, although, as she had increasing difficulty recognizing her mother in this ancient woman, perhaps it was someone else.

"Hello."

"Do I know you?"

"I'm your daughter."

"You know my daughter?"

"In a way, I guess I know her."

She didn't push. It just frustrated her mother, who shifted her gaze back out the window. A few minutes later, her mother looked at her again.

"Do you live near here?"

"I live in a small house, over by the ravine. Not too far."

"By the ravine? Just a bunch of hobos and hippies lived there in my time."

"Not much different now, I suppose. I've got a little land with the house, enough for a garden."

"Huh," her mother peered at her. "What does your mother think about you living with the tramps?"

"I don't know. What do you think she thinks?"

Her mother stared at her. "Do I know your mother?" Her mother's stare became very intense, searching. "Oh, yes. Yes, I know your mother, I remember her now. She comes to visit me from time to time."

They sat in silence.

What seemed like the time it takes to grow from an infant to adulthood passed before an aid finally came to signal the end of visiting time. Her mother looked in from the window again, this time at the intruder.

"Oh, hi there, Abby," she said. "This is my daughter. She moved back a few years ago. She lives with those hippies, the ones up by the ravine."

Then she faced out the window again, her face going blank again.

The woman with the beard left, thinking that, indeed, her mother did come to visit that ancient woman in the room once in a while.

The toad continued his introductory studies of the beginning and end of things with abecedarian eagerness, calculating the ratio of dripping sunflower resin, and watching the flowers that had closed at the end of the previous day slowly open to the new sun.

§

Nematode Garden Crisis

*"While most of the thousands of species of nematodes on Earth
are not harmful, some nematodes parasitize and cause diseases in
humans and other animals. Also, unfortunately, there are many
that attack and feed on living plants."* —OrganicGardening.com

The garden-shutdown, precipitated by a minority of garden
participants belonging to the Ancient Intransigent Nematodes
of Tea (AIN'T), shocked the woman with a beard. The
bleeding hearts cried soft nectar tears from their blossoms.

The toad flew in from a marsh in Africa to join a
meeting of garden life-forms. A few frogs chorused in
greeting as he joined. The snails still arrived last.

Only a small number of obstructionist nematodes instigated
the crisis. Their purported love of tea remains beside the fact.

They refused to participate in the interdependence of the garden,
insisting on withholding compost from the garden until all life
forms reformed the cycles of birth, life, death, decomposition,
rebirth through re-uptake by others—so only AIN'T would benefit.

Opposed to Socialist composting, they insisted that leaves,
cuttings, wintered stalks, and similar products, belonged
only to the seeds that produced them and their favored
worms, who re-processed them. They denied that soil,
other compost, rain, sun, air, or other symbiotic life-forms
contributed to producing these valuable food sources.

In short, they rejected biological interdependence with a parasitic
vengeance that threatened the ecological balance of the garden.

As far as their thinking took these worm-brains—
which was not very far, for, after all, they were
nematodes—as far as they could figure, the food
source belonged to the seeds that produced it.

The nematodes that processed
it, of course, took their take.

Their take on things did not agree with the
rest of the garden creatures' congress. AINT's
destructive-purposed refusal to participate in the
necessary budgeting of energy, time, and resources
to the process had now frozen the garden solid.

They had closed down the garden.

They brought December, but January
loomed ahead. Then the coldest temperatures
would penetrate deep into the soil. The
whole garden could collapse.

Without the protection of compost, the warmth
of its decomposition process, the absorption of solar
heat by its darkness—without the slight warmth
from this necessary system, the roots of all plants
would freeze solid. All of the seeds would die.

This did not bother the nematodes.

They didn't believe in January, climate change,
the cycle of life that produced the garden
or the inter-dimensional mathematical and
geometrical recursive reflections of its essence.

The worms only believed in eating what
they wanted for themselves and in a firm
denial of their reliance on others.

They pretended an interest in the seeds, but they
knew all seeds die when they grow into plants. They
did not care for the plants, despite AIN'T rhetoric.

The nematodes only wanted the
aftermath of compost to themselves.
And after the math, which they did not
understand, they only wanted for themselves
and their own everything they could
incorporate into their worm bodies.

The toad and a few bird friends feasted
on the AIN'T worms. The rest of the garden
life-forms worked together to dig the
compost out and to spread it on the garden.

Meanwhile, the woman with a beard
tried to recruit AIN'T nematodes
committed to interdependence.

The toad discouraged her, saying this
group were only soil pests anyway.

The toad flew to a marsh in
a Caribbean Rain Forest for the
winter in hibernation dreams.

The garden survived. Barely.

They were only soil pests anyway.

§

Political Philosophy

The woman with the beard didn't care much one way or the other about her hair, even though she preferred smooth-faced lovers. The morning bent like a knee toward the heat of the day. She sipped Coca-Cola slowly, just to please her friends.

Without warning, the filter of memory collapsed around her, a kaleidoscope of indecency exciting her erotic fantasies. Her lovers came back to her, their best orgasms, their lingering foreplay, each of their singular fires burning bright, like a comet in the night.

So she tossed the football around in her mind, catching it this way and that way until she dropped her hands to her sides.

At moments like this, the toad invited her to his garden. Mathematically imaginary numbers slipped into the square root of negativity while reeling fishing filaments through wrinkles of time-space reality. With the toad, it all came down to gravitational fields distorted by speeding photons collapsing time into.

No, she thought, stretched out in the lounge chair amid the sunflowers, tadpole pool, and morning glories. *Another mind experiment only leads to intellectual emptiness, a European philosophy of theoretical nothingness derived from envy of Buddhism.* Empirical error aside, the escape from metaphysics into socio-linguistic parameters scratched into the wall of a prison cell burned the flesh of the pan-hopping flea.

In the end, it came down to a group of industrialists and financiers attempting to overthrow Franklin D. Roosevelt and install fascism in the U.S., just before the Second World War. The scions of the conspirators followed the thread more patiently, the filament of time allowing three generations to do their work.

By the time the third generation arrived, the stars reflected across the waves of space-time, and the right-angled mirrors found smoke to create the necessary illusions. *Here*, she thinks, *we find the divergence of politics from history as it settles around the dust of religion.*

The politician she once shared a bed with died in a calculated plane crash for his sin of believing in the process. She still sometimes drops a tear or two for him.

She stopped worrying about all of this when she realized that the enemy shot real bullets through proxy warriors' guns. She didn't used to believe in conspiracy theories, then took them on as a cause, but now considers how to change the consciousness of the train wreck when the locomotives all have dead men driving them, hands grasping the dead-man's switch in *rigor mortis* tightness, while the radio controls remain set on kill.

Once, on her farm, she constructed a sculpture from discarded appliances, rusted tractor parts, car doors left on a junk pile. Walter Benjamin's Angel of History shoved car-discard wings against that train wreck we call progress. A bit of hose and a solar-powered fountain pump provided tears to drip down its face, over a bent fuel tank that resembled a gas mask.

When the politician came into her life, he insisted she had to take it down.

The electorate would rebel, he said.

Let them make war, she answered. *We'll make more than enough love to win.*

His plane crashed three months later. She pulled the sculpture down after the funeral.

Soon the Trumpets

A passionate green unfolds the toad's spring
garden into summer, but fades for fall into an
amber ambience about which the woman with
the beard broods each year. Somber, somnolent
season, this autumn beats the drums of winter
wars—a pulsing rhythm for the chilling dissolution
of carefully constructed order as flowers fall one by
one, vegetables unpicked plunge into inertia and
open their rotting cores to the world, and browns
dominate the frosted final frenzy of empires.

While only hints of this coming doomsday linger
in the morning chill as yet, still she recognizes
the call to arms—a struggle against chemical
pesticide invasions, a collapsing economy of over
productive zucchinis and under-ripe tomatoes
falling to waste in the developed regions of the
garden while the rich soil resources of its emerging
areas produce only mulch for the flowers.

Soon the trumpets on their vines will tout
technicalities that lead to war, the need for plows
and disks to pulverize the hard soil—pound
it to obeisance under the cold withdrawal of
winter, the depression of that mourning season
when the gardens lie dormant or dead before
the next spring suggests a new wing of empire
has started its agricultural March yet again.

This season she feels like joining those who
wish to ignite the end of time, to disperse into
an expanding space the contracting matter that
no longer discharges sparks. It could be that
sarin was a step too far, that only nuclear winter
can purify again. Radiation therapy for the
planet destroys the cancerous human cells.

Her anti-war days fall behind her, it
seems, or at least no longer conform to
uniform whiteness like blankets of imaginary
snow—its shadows, tints, and textures
erased. The glaciers melt at the poles, and
climate changes bring perspective to her
ideological calibrations. Sometimes resisting
winter, tenting the roses, composting the
tender roots and preparing the cellars
makes sense, and she would have done
that for every winter before now.

Sometimes the full details of differences
emerge in a more complex array of thought.
She could, this time, almost embrace
this chill in the air, the sense of finality, a
rounding to number three for the count of
recent peaks in the global conflict that has
not ended since the beginning of Western
colonization, even before: as the spice
routes collapsed and trade with Asia became
blocked, perhaps. Maybe reaching back to
the Egyptian-Greko-Roman empyriad.

Perhaps the pesticides in the garden,
introduced by a neighbor up the road, taint
her mind. Or maybe her aging in a declining
age raises this bellicose belligerence.

It doesn't matter in the end, she thinks
as she saunters down to the garden. The
universe doesn't much care how many lovers
she took to her bed anymore than it does how
many times this little planet dies and revives.

§

Ison Tonic Expressions

Ison, oh strange sky sound,
oh Ison, no bison, you
sound strange, Ison, in the sky,
scion of 4.6 billion years.

Workers ground the scraper
blade at odd hours, the cold air
vibrating the sound to wake
the dead or the living, who,
frankly, sleep more deeply than
the dead, especially Frank, who
with wonderment wondered
what wonder meant in the
face of such space sounds—
the end, the beginning, the
aliens strange at the door?

Knocking. Rumbling. About
to knock them over, or raise
them up, or play bowling for
dollars with the blue-green ball
third from the burning light.

No, just construction workers
it turns out. And, no, not the
sort that indicate that now is
the time to grab a towel and
a good guide to the galaxy.

But those other sounds? The harmonics, the rushing winds, the whistling whizzes of vibration and sibilance, consonance, melodic hints and abstract relationships? *Ah*, the woman with a beard considers, *what of those?*

She sits in the Toad's Garden contemplating the template of the sky and the whispering slithering sounds in the grasses, leaves fallen and crisped to signal the single slight movement of the world just above the soil and just under.

"What do you think? Soon Ison, perhaps the great comet of our lifetime, perhaps a dud, will swing by the sun."

The toad looks solemn and somnolent, past his hibernation (re)creation time situation, this winter hyper nation about to learn the chorus of the messenger choirs they imagine as trumpets calling an end note. They have no idea.

"Waiting is. It is not the first time," he says cryptically. "So, we wait again."

Around the world, the sounds echo in the sky. In Canada, in Russia, in Finland, in the United States, in Europe—for two years now— human ears could hear them, which should not be mistaken for understanding them or anything else much, for that matter.

The Apocalyptics have their triptych vision of angel choirs, end times, and renewal.

The Newly Aged sing songs of peace and harmony, oh water-borne aqueous ferment, peaceful planets and loving stars in the fifth dimension.

The Filmic think of *Close Encounters* of any kind, with a splinter group singing whale songs from *Star Trek* Intergalactic Shipping, Inc. A few ride the *Four Horsemen* into the ground, but they probably overlapped with the Apocalyptics. The future historians (aka Forwardians, as they will call themselves) later will debate this question, last week if all goes as predicted.

Paranoidsters stirred conspiracy mud: government piracy, secret brain control waves, and the likely overthrow of freedoms never meant to be given to advanced apes.

The Practical Non-Jokers explained and explained again, complaining of explaining.

Mostly, people did not pay attention to the strange sky sounds, these images from the night.

That is, other than Strange Sound Theorists working on obtaining tenure at academies of advanced advocacy for adhering to advanced advocacies advanced in career advancing and enhancing unreadable un-meant prose, who should remain unseen. And unread. Like this, perhaps.

The pilot named Nob thought, and the two-kilometer wide scout shifted two degrees. *We have to hit the corona of that star just right, rockaway. Otherwise we'll pull out of shape, or worse.*

Don't you think I know, rockaway scout ship number six-hundred sixty-six point six repeating six vibrated back. *My molecules are on the line, too.*

Nob shrugged internally. *After coming through so much time, I'm sure all our holistic system wants nothing more than to arrive at the transition point.*

It's clearly marked as the blue and green planet third from the star. Six-six-six point six-six-six repeating six scornfully scanned back.

Together, they sent the signal again.

We are coming. We return. Are you ready? Will you join us this time?

The woman with a beard and the toad listen to the audio borealis. The strange sounds convey time, echoes, and home. The woman with a beard watches the toad.

"Well, didn't you ever wonder why you could understand me? How I came to have this garden, about the geometric considerations of inter-dimensional semantic shifts in sheltered alcoves of the tadpole pool?"

She never asked such questions. In her experience, so many things remain unexplainable, and are usually better off left unexplained as a result.

"So, you will join them?"

"Not just me."

"Who else?"

He gazed at her.

§

The Palm Reading

The Palm Reading

Palm Reading
(As Far as I Go)

Out for a Walk

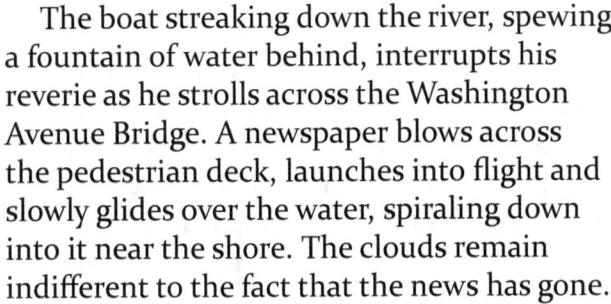

The boat streaking down the river, spewing
a fountain of water behind, interrupts his
reverie as he strolls across the Washington
Avenue Bridge. A newspaper blows across
the pedestrian deck, launches into flight and
slowly glides over the water, spiraling down
into it near the shore. The clouds remain
indifferent to the fact that the news has gone.

A ghost of unwrapped fish, the newspaper
floats until its print absorbs enough water
to drown the sorrows of its pages. It sinks
slowly as the Mississippi's current carries
it south, toward the ever distant Gulf. A
bicycle coasts by, two students debate some
ephemera of a course as they stride past,
three birds swoop to the railing and land.

Where had the frightened night gone, the
one weaving dreams through each flowing
day so that he could no longer tell mine
from not-mine and read minds of passersby?
What name, whose number, could look
him in the eye and not hear the evening
welcome up above the world so high?

He stands still, another tripper,
thinking, please, please make it easy, a
way out of the Sunday driver steering
his thoughts on a sight-seeing tour
without benefit of trampoline to catch
his horses as he fell through the hoops.

The hogshead opened its mouth, let the
apple drop, and played fair tricks with cards.
The kite soared above him as he jumped
on the trampoline, the horse jumped into
the ring, and the public failed to rise to
heed the call of the changing times.

Oh, let me walk and talk, he thinks,
like normal people do. I'd like to eat a
bowl of rice, put pennies in a jar, wash the
dirt out of my socks, without thinking of
Eleanor Rigby or Father Mackenzie as he
walks from the grave duty of visiting the
sick-in-the-head man he never knew.

Well, with only forty-six words in his
vocabulary, he prompted a revolution
among tattooed gymnasts trying to find
the right moves to unlock the *Kabbala*
on a good day. No miracles can save lives
now ready to depart their orbit, a polar
shift, the axis pointing to Texas as his
mind races to understand new meanings
for the woman with the beard.

Who can float in a river and not absorb the news that the course of time eddies and swells to the rhythms of unconscious rocks and debris strewn across the bed like his clothes the night he started to pack to travel to the Holy Land. Anointed by olive oil and dancing on the head of a pin, he realized the words of the Messiah were his own.

That's when he noticed that his voice was not his own, but belonged to the argot of Beatles songs, New Age tricksters, Holy hucksters, and frequent flyers enlarging their portfolios. *Call me Legion*, he thought, as the hybridity of socio-cultural construction work signaled ahead in the traffic lane below.

Meanwhile, he dog-legged logic,
coming to a hypotenuse-conclusion in
less time than it took for the tail to wag
the dachshund: entangled light provides
synchronicity through inter-woven
troughs and peaks of critical curiosity. He
need not move for generations, but his
message would change instantaneously
with each quantum shift and the legions
of messiahs would speak in unison.

That was then, this is definitely not now.
He continues to stroll across the bridge,
headed to the West Bank, watching the sun
set over the city. The flow of the river so
far below him soothes his anguished beast
of a mind with its seductive siren call.

72

He read in the newspaper that the
Palestinians and Israelis might sit
down to talk again, sometime soon.
One of their agents was overheard
saying "let's do lunch" to the other.

Hollywood is never stable, and
not even a stable of Hollywood stars
could produce a sure thing.

Hark, the Herald newspaper
continues. Another article reported that
still too few people observe Shabbat.
The Messiah has yet to come.

The comics weren't funny,
but the editorial page was.

And Nobody, the only politician to have kept a
promise, prayed for peace, knowing it would profit
Nobody. Only Wavy Gravy understood.

So, with these thoughts for his boat crew, he
found himself heading toward Cedar Avenue on
a cloudy day, sailing along in the breeze.

Palm Reading

You think you will eat *blancmange*,
you believe in bluebells from heaven, but
the gods have another story for men and
women, one twisted up with history and
boredom. One crashes ahead in chaos,
trying to restrain a train wreck with
broken wings, while boredom, always a
hog of the mind, escorts the boss to where
the rare models will dance tonight.

The palm reader looks into your hand as
the two of you sit on the pedestrian deck of
the two-level Washington Avenue Bridge.
Cars, trucks and buses on the lower deck
shake you in their race across the Mississippi
River, the Great Divide under you. She
traces your lifeline with her hand and
interprets it, a riot between wars and brain,
a brilliant kiss the only missing quality.

You wonder if she will serve you tea and
oranges that come all the way from China.

The water flows below, where
a poet jumped to his death when
the Minnesota winter overtook
him. It pours to the south at
a right-angle to the vehicles'
morning-to-night night-to-
morning rush, your slow amble
West, young man—magnetic
fields and electron flows
following the rules of thumbs.

That night you go to the bar
and don't notice, as you drink,
that a contortionist on the
beach in Negril weaves you in
his web a few years later. The
fire-eater breathes out over you
and a daughter not yet born.

Sometimes sixteen words or
maybe eighteen are enough.
Sometimes, it takes thirty-
six or maybe thirty-nine. An
inscription on the Abbey wall,
white stone burnished to cream,
like hearts beating on old
yellowed paper. At other times,
a deluxe revolver sings death in
staccato rhythms to a Caribbean
beat under the influence of the
frenetic tropical-night heat.

Oh pleasure, oh victim, as
the dynamite blasts open the
unconscious resistance, a big
headache that fights happy-family
mythologies to its dying day.

In other versions of this story, the travelers drink at the inn and argue drunkenly about trade, politics, religion, evolution, the NSA, the NRA, the CIA, DNA, and the ABCs of rock'n'roll. The dust settles around their boots, falling in clouds from their clothes and hair.

A dark-skinned dwarf enters, with no arms or legs. He somersaults his way into and around the room, and as he comes into focus, we notice a map of the world tattooed on his body, spinning in its own separate orbit.

This is how our lifelines unfold, what we find in the palms of our hands.

Riding the Chariot

A fiend roared within him, fueled by germs rioting throughout his system. They wanted more whipped cream, blue sex, smoke-filled rooms; they wanted more income, better homes, self-determination; they wanted democracy to rule his body. If he had a hammer, justice would rule with silver scales. The fool would lead them.

But bang-bang, the gavel falls, overruling his objections. The fiend takes over, and his cells and the germs war, killing each other and putting the community that one might think of as his body into perpetual motion.

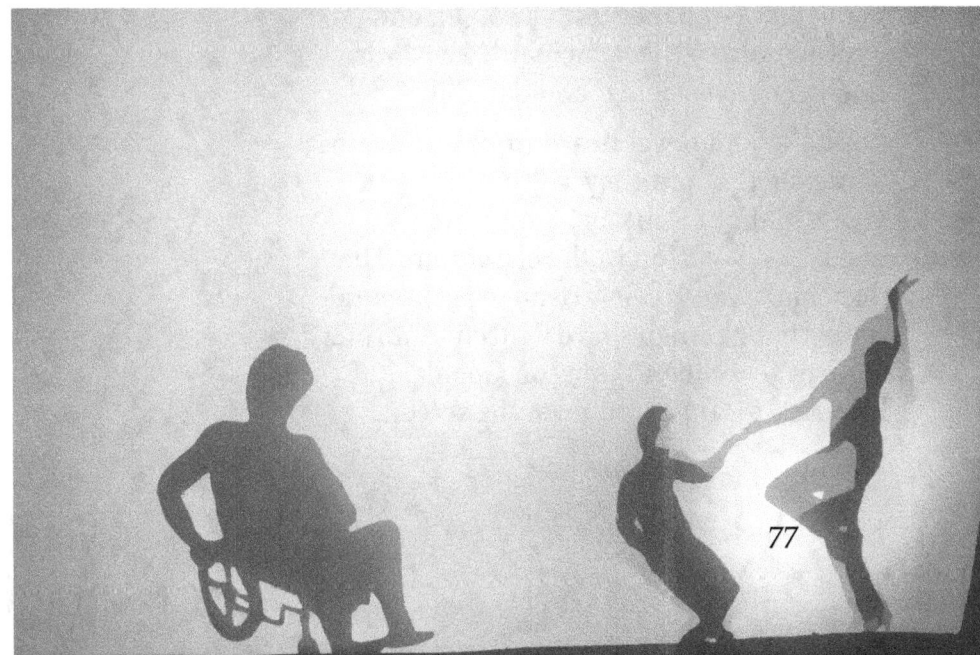

The teacher makes a scene for them
to memorize, part of the first act of
their lives. This is his job, to create neat
scenes for his un-dilated pupils to use to
construct a belief system and life to come.
He has long since listened to the critics
and realized the play will be a flop.

It all falls in on him when the
fiend takes over his body.

"Class dismissed. Go home, read
Rabelais, Larsen, Baldwin, Kerouac,
Morrison, Atwood and DeLillo. Write
an experimental novel. Go off the grid.
Build a life from your own materials."

The pupils stare at him intently,
comprehensively unable to stand under this
downpour, an outpouring of blinding insight.

"Seriously, once you have done that,
come back to me and ask for an A. Until
then, you have only failed, like me."

He walked out of the class. The 'flu
had won. He went to the office, pulled a
blank piece of paper from a copier, and
wrote a note to the principal. Two words:
I quit. Then he signed and dated it.

The school never heard from him again.
Someone thought they saw his name on
an essay about Rabelais, Freire and the
need for revolution in the classroom. The
principal read a review of an experimental
novel that he might have written. A former
student searched for him on Google, but
his name disappeared from the screen.

Walking the ravine ahead of angels, those messengers of shadowed new light, he forgot his mother. The trees painted, making art that lasted a mere second as a breeze brushed their shadows. With affection, he thought of an Aztec descendant he met in Machu Pichu. The land around him had a great thirst, not for rain, but for memory. A camera, hidden in a satellite, re-collected this moment of light bouncing from the rock party, a ball spinning on a pivot.

It made little difference to his views of the cosmopolitan metropolis instantiated in Berlin when the rodeo stopped in at the saloon. That poor raccoon, the gun, the Bible, the gin—you know the song. These thoughts swirled through the germinating revolution, the German revolution, the germ revolution, each a rival to his dreams.

They all tried stealing his sanity, but they found the vault empty, as he had discarded all previous construction materials, leaving a lattice of emptiness while seekers discussed the seven paths of mysticism in a courtyard around seventy-seven corners of relationship to the hole filled with rain. The wandering, colorful man no longer knew how to belong to the swimmers, so he stopped treading water, only to find that the water spit him out.

He felt silly, and thought of fixing it all, perhaps pulling the plug and disconnecting the hole from the screen. Still, a tired wink of his mind and his wonder returned, more quickly than the drink in the saloon arrived for the rodeo. His doctor thought he was depressed. His ex-girlfriend thought he was manic.

It could be bad, or better, if he only found what he needed to remember to forget. His skin would then refrain from thirsting for the rain, afraid that the world would fall from his shoulders, crash onto the pathless road; the wheels of the chariot would crush him with it. The soil would drink his memory. And the trees would brush over it all a surrealistic image, covering the sketch without any pentimento.

His dilated pupils did not like the new teacher. Their vessels expanded until they burst, exploding many myths at once. The principal was not their pal. They left school, but only after many years. They read theory. They taught in universities. They thought they were experimenting.

§

Blues Teacher

That night, he wrote a note to his doting students. In the note, he told them he needed to be free of them, so he was leaving, bye-bye to all that had gone before. The note stretched ego-dystonically to fit a not very harmonic blues melody line.

When he arrived at school early the next morning, he silently crept downstairs to his classroom. He taped the note to the white board that had long since taken over from the chalk boards that themselves had first been slate then replaced with green-paint. He left just as quietly through a back exit.

The less-doting students noticed the off-note right away and left for parts unknown immediately, disregarding the blues. The more doting waited for him to arrive, inexplicably late, before they acknowledged the blues and found the notice taped on the board, but missed the tone that rang just out of their range of hearing.

They stayed longer to discuss the matter. Yet it mattered little what they thought. He had left. They wondered what was the matter with him.

Then those grinds went back to work, imagining his lessons, assignments, and the grades given them. Thus, they graduated.

The blues still penetrated, and a certain melancholia infused the rhythm of their lives; a twelve-bar pattern emerged that shifted a minor-key across major-seventh chords, setting their thoughts adrift in a world of smoke, whiskey, and lost lovers.

§

Globalization

The Aztec calendar owned the land.
Sun and rain paid the rent, although
the camera she used to take the picture
zoomed in from some satellite, bouncing
its digital projections like a ball over
song lyrics at a sing-a-long party.

The point, or thesis of this exploration,
would pivot around ground zero gravity,
a sort of optical lens they all knew in
Cosmopolitan Berlin between the wars,
where another rodeo dancer at the
coffeehouse spoke American ex-pat French
to an Italian Bourgeois painter while at the
next table the Yiddish-speaking playwright
held forth on the Russian Revolution
now that he was beyond the Pale.

An actress who accompanies him nods
on cue during his monologues as they
travel the international Yiddish theater
circuit. Vienna next, then they travail in
London, Buenos Aires, New York—but
try to stay away from the Soviet Union.

A bull's eye tracks down Johnny-on-the-
spot, another satellite image telegraphed
into the train depot. Listen up, you gloved
foxes of the NSA, digitalis in too high
a dose poisons. The flower looks nice,
but watch out for the potentialities.

I don't know what you expect me
to write—a probability of narrative or
possibility of poetry or standard deviation of
sense—but if you peer through the spyglass
of Renaissance perspective you might find
yourself looking into the Eye of Horus,
hours ago sold to the highest bidder.

Free Masonry aside, all thirteen doves
flew the coup d'etat and haven't been heard
of since the renovations of the Annapolis
Chapel. The high priest, known as Rav
Cohen, suggests they have caught, sold, and
bought the Holy Dove. And will again.

So where do we go from here? To another
time and place where the clocks tick
irregularly and every one has a different
expression on its face. Some stop, some
go, some enjoy summer vacation—cations
fleeing solutions of unresolved inequalities,
dissolving into linear trajectories.

The NRA learned the Alchemists' secret
and turns weapons-industry lead into gold
everyday. The lobby of the sacred secular halls
never heard a whisper of democracy, and the
Iroquois shake their heads at the foolishness
of it all with Athenian smirks that would
weaken the Cheshire Cat as they wink and
hint at the decadence of Rome to come.

Try as I might to connect the dots, I'm
tired of being your ingenious djinni artist. I
want to lay down in the shade alongside the
woman with the beard and hear her story,
listen to the toad and the hairless tortoise revel
in revolutionary theory, speak with a lovely
lizard that crossed the street this afternoon,
and leave only a green nothing in my mind.

I forgot in my mindless state the codes
that unlock the cultural texts slipping
between the lines on my face, my palms
wrinkled into spiderwebs of uncertainty.

Look carefully at those signs. They reveal
a stranger scene than any I could write.
Someone, a painter, once told me the meaning
of the Aramaic. The potter spun his wheels.

In the lines of the date palm, watch as an inn fills with travelers covered in dust from a long day walking next to laden donkeys and camels. See them drinking and eating, talking loudly or quietly as may befit their mood.

A small, dark man has a map of the world tattooed over his whole body, but not just a map, for it is both a map and images from scenes of each place on the map, a stunning canvas we could imagine as greater than Bradbury's *Illustrated Man*. This man somersaults like a chariot wheel through the inn, down and up the uneven spiral-armed lacunae left around the travelers, and each revolution reveals whole new sets of images, a new possible world at each turn.

The travelers ignore the foolish gymnastic artist. The writer describes him incompetently and some reader becomes mired in deciphering. The effort of understanding turns elaborate, interactive sculpture into a few pencil sketches.

One or two of these sketches, left-over scraps from a feast of dreams, an old notebook nearly erased by light, distance, and time, remain suspended in our minds.

As Far as I Go

Mingled in dark hoops of time, moving
faster against lashes of space drawn out
then foreclosed as the speed of light
calls, casting shadows of reality into the
heat of the moment to cool against that
woman, *Eleanor Rigby*, who waits at the
window but doesn't answer the phone,
her breath condensed on the glass.

Well, *I just had to laugh and laugh* at how
much it looked like you, but it wasn't you,
was it? Still, we've met before, haven't we?
Look around, what have you got to lose?

We sit on this train, you think it's
just going normally along, but I tell
you, it's approaching light speed.

See how the green trees stretch, turning
brighter than all the colors of fall combined,
before giving in to brown as we pass through
sonic vibration into light incantation; spy the
houses and buildings blending into a long
blur of human construction, like a sentence
that goes on longer than a reader can recall,
abstract expressionism on a horizontal axis;
watch the wires along the tracks slide into
lines, a staff for your notes to harmonize the
melody of metals, set to the rhythm of the
wheels; observe this spatial expansion and
contraction related to the velocity of our hearts
as they beat, wondering what will transpire
before the next station stops all time and
space on a dime, your heart beat, mine.

See, I'm trying to tell you, *I'm just a station on your way, I know
I'm not your lover.* That sex we almost had in our imaginations as
you looked at me and I thought of you, that sex was the most fun I
had without laughing. And it would be again, if we laugh together.

And you? You, too, wake up each morning to the ground-
hog repetition of bedroom-community living, follow the money
and find the cheese at the end of the maze, Bob's your uncle.

I tell you, *you see that line down at the station?* We could slip out, just on our way, and disappear for an afternoon in a rented room, who would know? *I told you, I told you, I was one of those.*

Yet even as I tell you this, I watch you slip away. Who are you waiting for? Will he come to you today? Tomorrow? *I say hello, you say good-bye.*

You glance out the window, down at the floor, avoid my eyes and the words flowering out of my irises like bees to and from a blossom. I'm on the edge and falling off the edge and clinging to the edge with each word spilled over the edge, the cutting edge, slicing the thin remnants of sense and sensibility into the canyons. *Lover, lover, lover, come back to me.*

It doesn't matter. I'm *just another manic Monday* depressed Tuesday psychotic Sundae melting as I fly along the rails, keeping my foot off the live electric jolt of execution, waiting to hear from someone that, yes, this light-speed train compressed time to a point where we could expand into orgasmic eternity like back when smoking pot or doing a bit of acid and making love all night to a stack of vinyl records six feet tall.

No. No, officers, I wasn't
bothering the lady.

We were just talking, you know, about
physics and relativity and the prevalence
of mental illness among passengers of this
particular line. I spoke of soft seduction
and the early-twentieth century avant
garde so easily forged into ten-million
dollar fakes nearly a century later.

No, I don't have a line to use on her; no,
I don't snort lines of anything; no, I don't
mind walking on that imaginary straight
line on the platform as the train pulls away,
and I watch her eyes following me, longing
to be free, longing to join in the moment
of exploding suns and imploding stars,
black hole singularities denser than flour-
less chocolate cake at the high-end cafe in
that fancy hotel by Central Park, you know,
the trumped up dump owned by a dandy
lion escaped from the *Eden Express* zoo.

No, no, I won't be getting back on
the train today. I won't bother anyone.
This is as far as I go, the end of the
line. The 'is'—where I get off.

The Palm Reading

Off the Trail
(Dark Date)

Moshe's House in Space

Before, no sand swept through, no water
splashed—a beach at driving distance,
yes, but a long, long walk away. Before the
three-year old's stories, which I only half
listened to: he was born in clouds before
dinosaurs were alive; he died; "But now,"
he said, "I'm becoming alive again."

He told me he knew a dinosaur with bright
blue feathers and skin in the day. At night, he
said, it turned wooly and gray, to keep warm.
The dinosaur had a name, Pollaydowen. I
thought, what an amazing imagination my
three-year old son has, what colorful dreams.

He had other stories, about his house in
space and all of the animals that lived there
with him. How he had a farm at this house.
He went on and on with details—listing every
animal we saw at the zoo, on farm visits, in
books, on videos, on the internet; listing all
of the plants and flowers he had heard of;
listing creatures great and small in his lakes
and seas. How did he know all of them?

He insisted we should visit
his house in space.

Then changes came suddenly, not slowly, as even the most pessimistic predictions held. One day, news reports said the sea covered beaches even at the lowest tides. The next week, waves washed across roads. Houses washed away. Whole neighborhoods could barely evacuate before the surf swallowed them.

The water washed sand over everything. The ozone layer shredded. Paint bubbled and peeled on cars, houses, government buildings. Everything and everyone aged.

Sand dunes blew across where a road had run in front of our house. The house looked like fifty years of neglect.

The last day, my wife and I heard my son
speaking in his room. And another voice.

We went in. A bright blue flash turned toward us.

"We have to go," my three-year old calmly explained, "now."

"These sands end time here, the last to flow through the
hour-glass," the blue lizard-creature, Pollaydowen, added.

As we left the house, we trekked through hills of sand.

We returned once, to see what had happened.
I left this note for you, scratched in the walls, just
in case anyone remains. We have an ark.

§

Phone Safety

—the beginning of an unfinished story

Is it safe there? Are you okay?
She asks every time I call her.

No, I want to say. I almost got hit by a
car crossing the street in Tel Aviv. I was
in the crosswalk, the light was in my
favor, but the driver was in a hurry. The
drivers here, I want to tell her, are the
real danger. I have to watch out every
time I'm on the road; driving defensively
doesn't begin to cover it. It's like they aim
at you. So, you start driving offensively.

It's the aggression on the roads—the
constant horns, the lights flashing, drivers
screaming to get out of the way when there
is no place to move to and cars in front of
you as far as you can see. The cars that just
push into your lane, right next to you even,
without signaling, not that it would matter,
because you don't see the signal of a car
trying to occupy the same space your car is in.

Didn't these drivers study physics? Two
objects cannot occupy the same space,
no way, not at the same time. Ka-boom.
The universe blows up or something.

But this isn't what she means. Driving
is dangerous everywhere, she would
say. She worries. She means, don't
you want to come back home?

And insane driving isn't what I
mean. Maybe I am home, I guess, but it
doesn't always feel right. I want things
to be smoother, more gentle somehow,
more fair. But where is everything
fair? So, it could be that I'm already
home. I'm just not sure, though.

So, I say I'm safe.

Personal / Politics

He feels the fool. A soft doll, dressed
like a jester, the fool comforts him.

"Ooh," she coos. "A man
who plays with dolls."

He gestures with the jester just to her face,
not too threatening an approach, like a kiss.

"This is a serious political statement-
maker, this court jester is," he laughs.

"Politics are against the rules, dear lover."

"Jesters get to break the rules.
That's what makes comedians the
greatest commentators on society."

Sometimes, she thinks, *he goes overboard,
but on the wrong side of the boat.*

"No," she whispers, "enough
politics in bed."

But he doesn't hear her, or
maybe he just doesn't listen.

§

Independence Day

She didn't go to the fireworks
display that Fourth of July.

While eating breakfast, she noticed an article
on her tablet about the Freeloaders protesting
in Washington, D.C. The story reported that
they were all arrested safely, with no damage to
property and no injuries to working citizens.

Her mind wandered after reading this. A
few years ago, she had read in the paper, if you
still called it that, about the demonstrations
in a park. That was Turkey. In Egypt, they
demonstrated in the square. More than 30
million supposedly came out across the country.
Japan filled with demonstrators everywhere,
it seemed, from the photos. They protested,
what? Nuclear power plants, that was it.

She tried to tell her husband about this.

"People put their lives on the line everyday,
with those protests. And 1968, when students
took to the Paris streets. The Civil Rights
Movement and Anti-War movement in the
US also filled our news, with the March
on Washington and Chicago riots at the
Democratic National Convention that year,"
she reminded him. "Prague Spring was 1968.
Uprisings everywhere." Also, 2013. Occupy
Wall Street had excited her even before that
year. "But what had happened to all of that?"

He shrugged. "The Freeloaders took
to the streets instead of working to help
the country and our economy."

He never cared for news, she thought.
*He still prefers the sports section, but now
his nose hovers over his tablet instead of
inches from the newsprint and its smudgy
ink.* He liked his sports online, up to
the second, and approved for security
and safety by the NSA virus protection
and security software he'd installed.

His clothes fell in a rumpled mess
around his body, as though they had given
up on covering for him, and he looked
more translucent somehow. He still
drank coffee with lots of sugar and a little
milk. But he didn't take a second cup.

She returned to her musing.

It's been a long road, granted, but didn't people remember J. Edgar Hoover's wire tapping? CoIntelPro? Nixon's secret tapes? What about Operation Northwoods? No one other than a few easily dismissed academics seemed to know about, let alone care about, The Project for the New American Century, which called Sadam Hussein a convenient excuse to intervene in Iraq well before 9/11. The members of that think-tank filled W's cabinet and were well-known players in the whole escalation on the Middle East Front.

Not that we called it that, then. It was just the Middle East, she reflected, before we started to slowly change the language to acknowledge that this is another World War. Now, we volunteer to let the authorities listen to and watch us, asking for their protection.

Her husband looked up from his sports while her mind raced through this thin clothing over her even deeper conspiracy theories.

"Do you know what I remember about 1968?"

That he had thought anything about what she had said startled her.

"No, what?"

"Smoking pot, sex with you in my parents' basement, and skipping high school math class," he laughed.

She managed a smile. Yes, that, too.

"But in 1969, or was it 70?" She responded, "We were in our first year at Northwestern. We joined demonstrations at the Civic Center in Chicago, when they tried the Chicago Eight, remember?"

"I remember climbing up on the Picasso. I think it was the Chicago Seven, by then. They threw the Black guy out, what was his name?"

"Bobby Seale."

"Yeah. Him. The Black Panther."

She looked out the window. How had
it gotten to be 2020 already? It seemed
like an Arthur C. Clarke book title to
her, not a year in which she could live.

They looked at each other.
Where had it all gone?

"I'll tell you what," he continued.
"With the OPEC oil crisis, the economy
tanking, and all the bullshit that
followed, I'm just glad I found a job
when we got out of college."

She nodded absently. "Me, too. I
just wanted to build my career."

"And I'm glad we both have work,
now, too. Not like the Freeloaders
out there," he added.

"It's not like they choose
to be out of work..."

"Only so many jobs. Those who
try, though, they get them."

Here it was, July 4, Independence Day. They woke up, checked into the NSA portal on the computer, and listened to the house alarm deactivate. They ate their breakfast. Soon they would go to work, him at a cyber-defense contractor, her for a global marketing firm, both helping to keep the world markets open for America's businesses.

This was the goal, so that they, the workers, could survive. Enemies threatened America, destroying jobs and job opportunities, so Americans had to defend the economy to protect their lifestyles. *The sacrifices had been tremendous*, she thought.

"I'm not sure it was worth it," she muttered.

"The demonstrations in the 60s?"

"No. Giving up so much."

"Look around you. We have jobs that pay well. We have a nice house, a green yard. Our kids have their houses; our grandkids go to good schools. We have it all. What did we give up?"

She gazed at him. He looked more than ever like a ghost to her.

"Meet you at the fireworks tonight?" She asked as she got up from the table.

"Sure," he nodded, turning back to the tablet computer in front of him as she left the house.

She didn't make it to the fireworks. She just disappeared from his life. The NSA tablet tracer software and the GPS in her phone located both at her office.

"We think she left, joined the Freeloaders," they told him.

Somewhere in the back of his mind he wondered, did she?

§

Off the trail

By chance I learned that they planned to crucify the married couple for honeymooning off the grid and outside the mainstream economy. The couple backpacked along the Appalachian Trail, using second-hand equipment, carrying home-prepared dried goods for meals , which friends provided to them as gifts.

The followers of Christ Capitalist found such sacrilege untenable, especially in light of the anger it would cause the Corporate Lords of the Boardrooms.

I heard my editor on his cell, assigning someone to cover the Meeting of Judgment where the sentence would be pronounced. When I overheard that the other reporter wouldn't be back from her current assignment in time, I sauntered in and asked what Ed had for me, like I didn't know anything.

"The Reverend called to request we send someone to this meeting, give it coverage to send the message out. Work, spend, play inside the economy."

"Got it. Keep the money flowing."

I knew the catechism, but didn't believe it. I'd sent dried lemon peels, home-made penne (dried to preserve it), a chunk of parmigiana traded on the underground market, and a sealed container of pesto for them to make a backpacker's lemon pasta.

The Meeting of Judgment followed the usual pattern of these religious courts. A minister of the Reverend's flock read out the charges. Two other ministers sat on either side, listening gravely. They conferred briefly. It didn't matter that the accused even now were somewhere hiking in the woods.

As per custom, the ushers served cups of tea to the witnesses at the Meeting. I sipped a sad orange-pekoe until the lead minister announced a decision.

Crucifixion. It had come back in style around 2020, shortly after the great purges that deported, jailed, or enslaved first the non-Christians, then the wrong-type Christians.

I had not seen a crucifixion. Up to now, it had been an advantage of a rural assignment.

"What are you going to do?" The man I knew as Germaine asked me. He'd popped up out of the crowd as I pushed out the door.

I'd seen Germaine at several social gatherings of people like me. My circles went along with the Reverend to a point, that is, enough to survive, and no more. We kept to ourselves, and tried to avoid the scrutiny of the Reverend and his ministers.

"Do? I'll write a story about the Judgment, the reasons for it, and watch to see how many hits it gets on the Screens." I didn't know Germaine enough to be baited into saying something damaging. Besides, that was what I planned to do.

"No, about them. We can't let them get caught."

"You could get crucified yourself for getting involved. Even what you said is a crime against Christian Capitalism."

"What is Christian Capitalism? Something made up by corporate overlords. There never was such a religion."

I walked away. I considered whether he might be an agent provocateur, meaning I should report him before he denounced me for doing nothing. I decided that I didn't want to get involved, and would invoke my sometime role as investigative reporter should he accuse me.

The next morning I had coffee with Frank, someone I thought I knew enough to trust under most circumstances. He told me that Germaine had been arrested for sedition, blasphemy, heresy, all as a result of spouting the Devil's own socialism.

"I'll be damned."

"Probably," Frank said. "To tell you the truth, I thought he was a spy."

After Frank went off to work, I looked for a story on Germaine, but didn't find one. I wondered how Frank had heard.

I read my story on my Screen. It played well, several hits, re-posts, and praiseful comments.

It bored me. No, more than that. It sickened me.

I didn't believe any of it. I knew the young couple, knew they loved the woods, knew they couldn't afford a resort honeymoon because they wanted to buy a house and the downpayment would take everything they had.

They wanted to fit in and had no revolutionary or irreligious intent. They just wanted to get along.

Just then, I realized that the Reverend and the ministers didn't care. And maybe Frank didn't read about Germaine on a Screen.

The Reverend wanted to make a statement, keep people scared, keep people trying harder than ever to feed the economy and concentrate power and wealth into the Corporate Lords, who ran the Reverend.

Or maybe the other way around, the Reverend ran them. It doesn't matter now, I realize.

Frank wanted me to play along and keep away from people like Germaine. It was almost a friendly gesture.

And that's why I find myself sitting in a deer stand along the Appalachian Trail. The newlyweds should pass under it sometime today, if they haven't yet been waylaid.

When they do, I'll wait to see if they find the package I left out.

It has printouts of the Screen story I wrote. It has a copy of the Judgment Decree. It has a map of little-known trails that cross this path, and what cash I could withdraw without getting stopped by a minister.

I thought that I would watch them pick it up and wait until they were gone, then make my way home after a few stops to justify my travel, should I get checked.

Now I'm thinking maybe I'll ask if I could walk with them a while when they go off the trail. I'll cut out after a few days, find my own way.

I don't know why I've decided to do this. I just don't feel like writing another story I don't believe in, I guess.

§

A Warm Gun

The rain dripped without enthusiasm,
barely wetting her head as she slipped out
of the car and up the front walk. She might
almost have escaped detection, except for the
man across the street standing out of the rain
under a store's shade canopy. He watched
her enter the house then walked away.

She entered the house without
making a commotion. From upstairs,
she could just make out a few sounds.

Creating little noise herself, she walked to
the kitchen, opened the refrigerator, took out
a carton of pretend lemonade, pulled a glass
from the drain board, and started drinking it.

It was not her house, her
glass, or her lemonade.

She sat at a table in the kitchen,
finishing the fake lemonade. She wished
the almost-rain would fade and give way
to sunshine. It didn't, though. The rain
seemed just a cliché, but no matter.

She waited a bit more, then set the glass
in the sink and made her way up the stairs.

From his bedroom, she heard a
murmuring of voices. Two voices, no more,
no less, but she couldn't quite tell whose.
She opened the door without knocking.

He lay naked in the bed, of course.
This is what you and she expected.

His lover was a gangly man, wearing a half-slip and nothing else. You might not have expected this, but she wasn't surprised. The writer of this little fiction tended to bend gender expectations as a trope or theme, she wasn't sure which it was.

She was surprised that it was her slip the lover wore. She must have left it here last weekend. Then, she thought, perhaps not. Perhaps one of them had taken it from her place.

You would expect her to make a scene here, an argument to ensue, jealous words thrown in spite. She would have thought that would be her reaction, too. But, no, the writer took a different path. So, she looked at the scene in front of her and laughed, shaking her head.

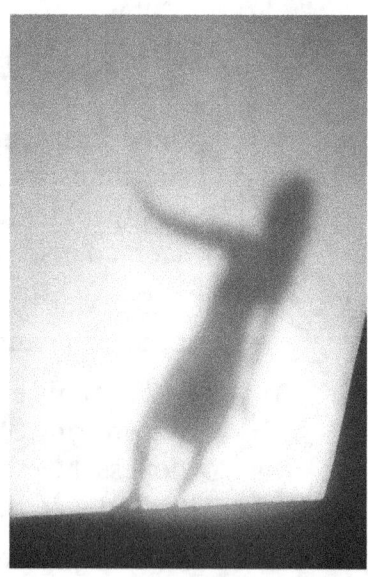

"Am I the beard?" She asked.

"It keeps the Company satisfied. No fags allowed."

"Ah. Well, I think that I'll shave now, if you don't mind."

She walked to the closet, pulled off a few items she had left there, then over to the dresser and grabbed a few things that were hers from a drawer.

"You can keep what's in the bathroom—souvenirs, or camouflage, whatever. Oh, and keep the slip. I don't want to think about the warm gun that just fired in it."

And she went downstairs, out the door. She dropped the key in the mailbox.

She did not notice that the man, who had stood across the street before, now sauntered down the sidewalk on her side of the street. As she unlocked her car, he walked up to her.

"That was quick for a lover's tryst," he said.

She looked up, startled. He looked too corporate somehow. Company.

"Tryst tonight. I just needed to pick up a few things for the cleaners," she spat, tossing her bundle into the back seat. "Not that it's any of your fucking business."

"I'm jealous. I thought he'd be with me tonight."

"I doubt you thought any such thing, if you ever think. Anyway, you're not his type, I assure you." She ducked into the car, started the engine, and drove off without waiting for a reply.

This isn't the end you expected. She
didn't like it, either. She thought that
it would be nice to weave some sort
of sense from all of this. She shouted
at the writer that he was an idiot.

"It's a political caricature," she yelled
in the car, "a bit of argument against
corporate control of our private lives and
the complicity of the government."

And, it bent her life out of shape without
any concern. Her body had to absorb the
lies against it. She may not have been in love
with him, but she thinks it's possible. Why
else did she leave so calmly, and protect him?

No, she didn't like being a
character in this story, not at all.

The other man who betrayed her—not
the writer— didn't mind. His part was
small—a silly moment in bed with another
man wearing her slip. He might move up
from this sort of part, get something good, a
supporting role in a novel, perhaps even be
the hero. Or anti-hero. It's all good for him.

The man in the slip didn't have any lines,
and didn't care either way about the story. It
was another fiction gig. He wanted to make
it in poetry, something erotic and romantic.
Maybe a poet would notice him here.

She, however, remained stuck in the
role of the betrayed lover who takes it
well. The sensible woman. The Victim.

So, she stopped the car just after that ending. She turned around, nearly hitting two cars, and drove back. *It's like an action movie scene*, she thought.

This time, she noticed the man standing under the awning.

She reached into her glove box and pulled out a small automatic pistol. It doesn't matter what brand, the company won't send this author the best model to add to his toy collection, and they certainly don't care about her. Let's call it a Chekhov.

It's a good thing that she, at least, went to the firing range and learned how to shoot. Well, maybe not so good for the other characters. Perhaps she's an enemy assassin, after all.

She stands up straight when
she exits the car, lifts her arms up,
pointing at the Company geek, and
fires three rounds into his chest.

She goes up the sidewalk, pulls the key
back out of the mailbox, and lets herself in.
The men stand on the stairs, lover with a slip
looking out to the right, the liar checking
down and to the left, guns pointed.

"Did you hear the gun shots?" Her
faux-boy friend calls out. "Get down."

"Sorry boys. I don't own a silencer." She
shoots the remaining six shots in rapid
succession, three into one, three into the
other, all closely grouped near the heart.

She reloads. Then she aims at the story and blasts
all nine bullets into it, putting it out of its misery.

Unfortunately, she misses the writer.

§

Dark Date

The polyethylene toy didn't last long, which was a drag. They never last long, you barely get them out of the bag before they come apart at the seams or a bit breaks off. The kid gets his hand on them, and they're done for good, all in pieces within the time it takes to blink. He should probably have brought something more substantial for the little brat. Maybe a pair of jackboots so he could look the little tyrant he acts. No matter. Not much time left anyway.

"Sorry he broke your present," she offers, looking nice in a kilt-like plaid skirt. "Alfred can get a bit rambunctious when he's excited by a new toy."

"No problem. I should have gotten the sweet boy something more sturdy."

"No need to bring him anything, you know." She kisses him on the cheek.

If only it were so, but he knows better. The toll for entry to her house and life was paid directly to the kid.

"You're so sweet to both of us," she continues. "Thanks again, for giving up last weekend to fix the stove."

"No problem, just a little electrical wiring, and great company."

They say good-bye to the babysitter
and the boy and head out the door;
she takes a last glance in the looking-
glass in the entryway as they depart.

Walking down her block, they
look for any empty taxis, finally
landing one after a few minutes.

"I saw your picture in the newspaper,"
she tells him as they settle in the backseat.

"Ah. That reminds me, I should
wear better ties on court days."

"Well, you looked handsome."

He smiles at her. Handsome
is as handsome does. And if she
only knew what he did.

"What?" She prods.

"Another day, another lawsuit defended."

"You seemed to be thinking about
something serious, darker."

He laughs. "Well, I'm really a serial killer
of divorcées and their sons. I was just trying
to figure out how to catch you unawares."

She grimaces, then laughs. "You
have the darkest sense of humor
of anyone I've ever met."

Tonight felt right.

The cab drops them by the river. He had suggested a romantic stroll for the last few blocks to the restaurant where she expected a pre-theater meal.

The papers later describe it as a freak accident, a horrible family tragedy. The divorced mother, on a date with her new fiancé, fell off a pedestrian bridge into the river and drowned. Several witnesses saw her lose her balance, him grab for her but just miss catching her as she tumbled over the railing.

And on the same night, while police and rescue teams pulled her from the river, the house with her son and the babysitter in it burned down, both dead. The electrical fire could have killed them all at home. Some people speculated about the nature of fate.

Her grieving fiancé savors the sympathy, wearing his new tie at the double funeral as the cameras flash. *Next time*, he thinks, *will have to be much less public*.

But what a kick, what a story.

§

The Palm Reading

Final Destination
(A Crack in Everything)

Character Development

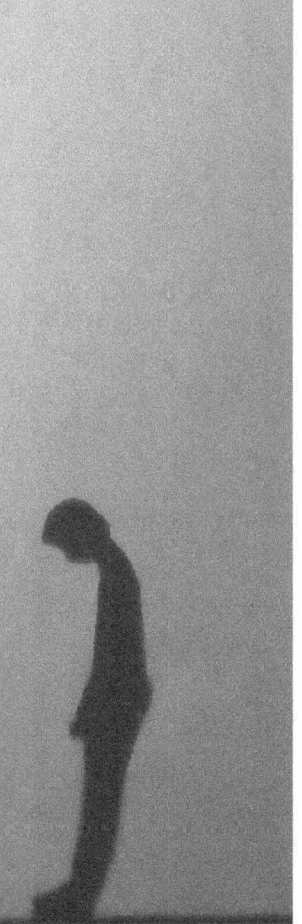

His book does not draw me into the garden. He does. So many people milling about inside, talking about him and the book. He stands out here, by himself, with a drink in his hand.

Warm air cozies up to the flower heads as he stands there, waiting for me. Or so I imagine. He sees me coming. He thinks it's safe, but he's wrong.

"How was yesterday at the beach?" I ask, nonchalantly sipping my bourbon on the rocks.

"We saw a lot of starfish in the tide pools."

"Did you know that if you cut off one of their arms, a new one grows right back?"

"Is that so?"

"I read it in a book. It was better than yours. The book."

"Oh."

"I've always wanted you."

"Really? For what?"

"You won't let your marriage get in the way, will you?"

He looks stumped.

"In the way of what?"

"Our affair."

"What affair?"

"The one we're going to have. I want you to be my lover."

"What was wrong with my book?" He asks desperately.

"Nothing."

After a few awkward minutes, he says, "Your wife wouldn't like it if we had an affair."

"Neither would yours. They can grow new arms."

"I'm not sure I follow you."

"I wish you would follow me. Pay attention. Preferably, to me."

Some other guests join us outside. I wish him happy birthday in my most manly voice, then drift back inside. I catch him stealing glances throughout the afternoon.

The next evening, most of us from the party attend the official event, his reading at a trendy bookstore across the river. The reading that will launch a thousand books, you might say.

He starts out straight enough, reading a selection from the opening chapter of his new, current novel.

After polite applause, he announces that he's started a new work just today. He thinks it would be exciting to share some of the novel-in-progress, he says.

"My friend told me that she did not like my latest book at all," he begins. "Then she propositioned me over vodka martinis. It was a noisy, crowded cocktail party in a fashionable apartment on the Upper Westside, full of loud people who don't listen much, the party well underway that late in the evening, so I doubt anyone heard besides me.

"This was right after a discussion of starfish regeneration, and I wasn't sure I had heard her right. Starfish can grow back an arm, if they lose one to a predator. When she told me that, I wondered if somehow my heart could grow back, if I could learn to feel again, since I had lost it to a predator so long ago.

"She stood there, so sexy, lovelier than the Master's Margarita, perhaps as lovely as a Magritte. So, when she asked me to be her lover, I could have projected those words into her mouth. And I wanted her. So, I boldly said, 'yes.'

"That began an affair doomed by science, predators, and broken-off arms. But this story is not about that, or her, or me. It is about you and it is about the storyteller telling."

This new book is better, I think.

§

Character Actor

He always thought he was a loner,
but he always liked to have a woman at
his side, preferably wearing high heels
and a top with a low-neck. And he
wanted other men to see her there.

His mother called him in California once
a week and they chatted about nothing for
ten minutes or so before saying goodbye.
She gave up on asking about details of
his life when he was in high school.

They spoke mostly about the weather,
sports, current events, and a bit of gossip
about his old friends she'd picked up from
the neighbors back in Hopkins, Minnesota,
where the grass was always greener.

The woman sleeping next to him at
the moment seemed sweet, but his heart
wasn't in it. It never was. She stirred.

He got out of bed, dragged a comb through his thinning hair, and went to the kitchen. He didn't make her a cup of coffee, so she made herself one when she stumbled in a few minutes later.

"I think it's time to move on," she said as she added milk to her cup.

"Yeah, I know what you mean."

"This is kind of a shallow life you live, don't you think?"

"It suits me."

"I guess."

"Must suit you, too. You play the game."

"It's a game?"

"Isn't that what the movies call it?"

"I keep thinking maybe one of you guys will stick. The spark will ignite, you know?"

"You mean like fireworks in bed?"

"No, more like a blaze of glory—fame, fortune. I think, maybe you'll land a movie part that sets you up for stardom, all of that."

"I don't act."

"Okay. But maybe you'll write something, a book that gets optioned for a hit movie. We could have a couple of mansions, live the big life."

"I don't write."

"What do you do?"

"Mostly I screw around, wait tables when I have to, do odd jobs around town for shady characters when I can."

"Sounds like a character actor."

"Yeah, that's me."

She shrugged.

"I want a leading man."

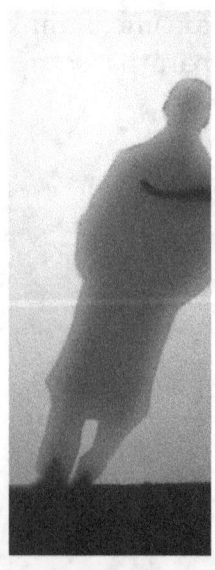

After breakfast, and a little morning-good bye screwing, she clicked out of the house. Her high heels glittered. The low-cut blouse ruffled in the breeze as she wheeled her overnight bag behind her.

He watched her from his bedroom window, scratching his balls.

A character actor can get steady work, he thought, and shrugged his shoulders. Maybe he would audition.

§

The Big Sale

A clean day, she thought, on her way to work. Perhaps it's a sign that her big customer would come in today. The train clacked its way through busy suburban mornings, workers on the platforms under waiting skies.

Her life of a realtor, a bedroom community commuter, bored her. She once wanted to paint. She wrote a bit now, mostly in the evening after supper. She dreamed of becoming a sculptor, forming metal with her torch in hand.

Perhaps, when the big customer came, the sale that would let her walk away from real estate, then she would rent a studio.

She adjusted her skirt as she shifted in her seat. Out the window she saw an anonymous street, people waving good morning. She didn't know the low-down on the characters or what tea the men's wives found okay, but she could read the pantomime. The train moved out of the indistinguishable station, closing the show before the reviews came in.

The man across the aisle nodded at her before turning back to his cell phone updates. Apparently he had observed her watching the street, imagined a shared consciousness. She wondered what went through his mind, what was different from her own musing, if any one thought was the same or even similar.

He didn't seem like much: rumpled suit, standard smart phone, suburban-dead eyes that might hold a small glint of fantasized adultery. She figured him for an accountant or insurance adjuster.

At her stop she saw him getting up, too. He smiled. She restrained from giving him a grimace, but couldn't bring a smile.

Drinking her coffee at her desk a short while later, she checked her email again. Nothing new.

The man from the train came into the office. They recognized each other, of course.

"I'm, um, looking for Amanda Moyer?"

"You've found her," she went into full professional mode. "How can I help you?"

It turned out he had found her
name in a listing for a high-end condo
overlooking the river. He wanted to see it.

"I guess most people call. I like to see
the person I'm working with, though,
before they know we'll be working
together. Old fashioned, I guess."

"You didn't follow me on the train, did
you?" She tried to laugh it into a joke.

"No, no. I'm living out in Glendale
temporarily. Until I find a new place."

Divorced, it turned out, and he'd
been renting. Now he wanted to settle
in, buy a place. Financing wouldn't
be a problem, he assured her.

He didn't like the first condo, but agreed
to see another one she told him about.

"The price is higher. What
range are you looking in?"

"Price isn't a problem."

He wasn't an accountant or insurance adjuster. He had sold a high tech start up for a number with more zeros than Amanda could count.

He bought the fifth condo she showed him, a very expensive one, so he indeed was her big customer. She could have walked away and lived on the commission for many good years, bending metal every day.

But she didn't.

§

A Day in the Life

Somewhere, he knows, a bed waits for him to drop into it.

The comb falls from his hand onto the counter by the sink.

This buy-and-sell life reflects in mirrors distorted by smoke, creates a dream that fills a cup with desire. The cup, therefore, remains empty.

The Knight of Cups, dragged upstairs from slumber near The Fool, turns the tables on us all.

What tabled dream, a comb pulled through hair in bed, smoke and mirrors, a cup dragged from the upper cabinet and taken upstairs—what dream un-debated, un-voted on, empties his will into an automaton of desire?

Somewhere a bed waits for him. He drops in it without seeing. It's in the film, the one where they win the war.

When he wakes, the room has
already filled with the heat of
the day. He struggles out of bed
from restless sleep, stumbles into
the bathroom, combs his hair
again. Smoke drifts in his mind,
clogging the memory of the
dreams that make him so weary.

Downstairs he downs a cup of
orange juice, then sips his cup of
coffee while reading the paper.
The news dragged on, making
him long for his bed upstairs.

The film review reminded
him of a book he'd read
a long time ago.

>
> Upstairs, she woke beside the
> depression that he once filled. The room
> held more heat than his indentation.
>
> She fell out of her side of the
> bed, rolled downstairs.
>
> "Morning," she mumbled.
>
> "Off to work and what do you get?
> Another day older, deeper in debt."
>
> "Yeah. Another song, got the
> words all wrong," she countered.
>
> He slid a cup of coffee across the counter
> to her, kissed her cheek, and left.
>
> She thought he looked familiar,
> when he kissed her cheek.

She showered, dressed, and sat at the table with a bowl of cereal, reading the paper. A car accident, fatal, apparently—the driver went through a red light. The photograph revealed his face from a few years ago. She'd seen his face before. Just before he went out the door.

The clock informed her she was running several days late, so she grabbed her hat and coat and ran for the bus.

That evening, she came home alone to her empty flat.

The dreams would swallow her again tonight. All those holes, so small, filling up nothing like as big as the Albert Hall.

The dreams would spit her out in the morning.

Maybe she should move to Blackburn, Lancashire.

§

Why she was late for dinner...

A bag falls to the sidewalk, glass shatters, wine spills—a ghost woke and walked by her, a forgotten moment now scented by shiraz evaporating on hot cement. These days she simply shrugs off such occurrences—hidden minutes pour out along her path wherever she goes, a seam split in a pair of too tight jeans, she supposes, a transcribed protocol. The specter turns, grins at her, a hungry leer that imagines he knows her sexual desires but reveals by its grimace that he remains clueless even about his own fantasies. He would try to turn her brown eyes blue, given the chance to experiment on her. He turned into the middle of the street and disappeared as though around a corner. She looked at the splashes of maroon around her. A painting fell out the window of the third floor of an apartment building, tumbling end over end, revealing Rorschach images in light green before cracking on the short garden wall near the entrance and bouncing to a stop at her feet, where the canvas absorbed the wine stains. Port-wine birthmarks stain her inner thighs just where the smooth skin begins to tingle when she wants to kiss a lover. She picks up the bag, carefully sliding the broken shards back in, and throws it out in a trash receptacle on the corner. With her hands empty, she calls to explain that she will arrive late for dinner. When she enters a liquor store to buy more wine, she meets an old girlfriend. Her friend tells her that she had died in a car accident a few months before and recommends the merlot—mellower than the shiraz. Dinner turns out well, a warm meal with good company and lots of laughter. She doesn't tell anyone that she sees the past dancing in the shadows, the present always remains a bit out of focus, and the voices speaking to her and only her come from the future. She just appreciates the mellowness.

§

Open Road

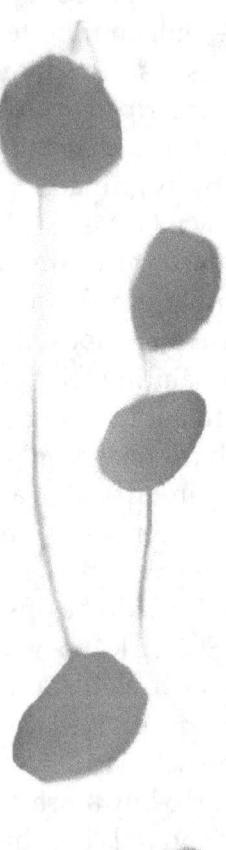

She lifted the weight of his head
from her pillow. It surprised her with its
lightness. All this time, she thought it
would be too heavy to move, a dead weight
murdered by an invitation to love.

She took a break from her labors,
quit her job and stuck her thumb out
for a ride, figuratively speaking. In time
someone picked her up at the bar, but
she got out at the next corner after his
whiskey breath became unbearable.

The next day she woke up alone, the pillow fluffed without the indentations of past lovers. She felt joyous, danced out into the street and skipped down to the coffee shop. Double-shot latté and she roared down the road out of town.

This took her to the beach on a foggy morning. Shreds of litter caught in the seaweed amid the strips of kelp and bits of broken shells. She held a mirror to herself and stripped down, swum naked in the cold sea.

When she got out a man stood there, but she ignored him. He watched her get dressed, her wet skin soaking her clothes.

"I've got a heater in the car," he said.

"I've got one in my glovebox, and I know how to use it," she replied.

He looked blank, but her gun was loaded. He turned away.

She drove up the coast until the state line, crossed over into a new consciousness and later slept in her car by the side of the road.

She found that even without her telephone, she did not want to die. In the morning, she opened the steamed windows and took a peep at the dawn. She drove to the first fast-food stop and bought breakfast on the go, without even opening her door.

Love should be like this, she thought. Not the lie of fairy tales and romantic comedies, but the road-story love, a stoney path underneath the moon where you could stumble and fall before the light would penetrate deep enough that you yourself radiated into the night.

No, that was the same trap, she realized. She just wanted to keep on riding down this road, wherever it would take her.

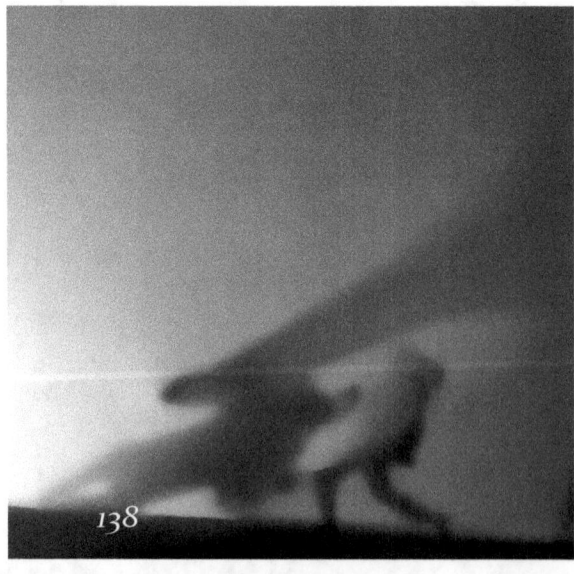

138

She called him about a week later,
told him she was alive, all was well, he
could sell or throw out her stuff.

"When did you leave?"

She would have told him never
mind, but he didn't anyway, so it
would have been redundant.

"Before you woke up, about a week ago."

"Oh."

"Didn't miss me, I guess."

"You know, we're rehearsing.
It's all about the movie now."

"You're a life-draining emotional-
energy hog, did you know that?"

"It's the part. Method acting is like
that. We start shooting next week."

"The script sucks."

She likes her new screenplay
much better. She thinks of
shooting him in the movie,
but knows it wouldn't
be worth the effort.

§

A Crack in Everything

Dinner with my sister
Alice always involves a drink.
Or drinks. It helps us get
through the occasion.

So, tonight I've got single-
malt scotch in my hand, not
sure what brand, but positive
that I couldn't afford to buy
it. I sit on the sofa and watch
her with her friends—lawyers,
stock brokers, marketers, a
mid-level bank officer or two.
To me, they are just names and
faces from another dinner.

When I take my leave for a few
moments to use the facilities,
I notice that the bathroom
mirror remains cracked. This
surprises me. The mirror
has been broken for over six
months. That it remains broken
doesn't fit with Alice's tidy life

and nearly obsessive neatness.
Any nick or dent in anything,
and it's trashed or replaced.

I sometimes worry that she
will replace me. Or, given that
adopting a middle-aged brother
in your own middle-age might
not be realistic, perhaps my
worry is more that she will
trash me. I mean more than
with words, something she
does often and with relish.
I think she might literally
throw me out with the trash.

Some of my nicks and
dents show. Small scars, bags
under my eyes, wrinkles,
graying hair, a deep weariness
that drags me into torpor.
Everyone can see it in me.
*Here's Uncle Joe, he's a'movin'
kinda slow, at the junction...*

Most of the imperfections do not surface, but hide deep. Alice doesn't mind shining a light on them, though. When she's had two drinks, she starts with the spotlight, for anyone who will listen in this crowd or among family (none of whom, other than me, were invited to this particular soiré). When she's had four, she slows down and becomes more interested in her guests, especially the wealthier and more good-looking among them—either men or women, *machs nicht*.

She is on her third drink. I am on my second. I hear her in the other room as I creak my way up the hall, returning from the bathroom.

"His second so-called book of poems? Do you know how many sold? Not even fifty. Why does he persist? There's no profit in it."

I sense as much as see heads nodding assent as I enter; an only slightly embarrassed hush falls over her audience as they awaken to my presence. They pointedly look away from me to Alice, the person next to them, or someone across the room.

Alice carefully arranges everything from cocktails to dessert. At dinner she has set me down between two unmarried women—a divorced social-media marketer (whatever that is) named Janet and another woman, Yvonne, whom I recall at another of Alice's dinner parties expressing a vague interest in writing.

By the time dessert comes, Yvonne has turned to the man on her left. She likes novels, apparently, preferably thrillers or romances. Presumably her taste in writers follows suit, that is, not my suit, which is a bit threadbare compared to the rest of this crowd.

Janet has hung in with me, explaining social media, engagement, conversion, search-engine optimization. The English language seems full of words that I thought I knew the meaning of, but which apparently have taken an online turn that I didn't follow.

"What you need to do," she holds forth, "is market yourself. Make you and your poetry into a brand. You need to define your mission, tell your story, sell yourself."

"You mean like a movie star?" I ask politely.

"Exactly. Or a best-selling author. It's all about projecting personality. You have to build followers, have people friend you, and post interesting things. That's what will convert to book sales."

"I write poetry," I say, and wonder when friend replaced befriend as a verb.

"Well then, define your audience. Probably other people who write poetry. Who else buys poetry books?"

"Readers of poetry?"

"Nobody reads poetry. Do you have an eBook I could download?"

I shake my head. I know about eBooks, at least, but I can't help thinking that they're several steps below a B-movie. I mean, there is no E grade. The scale goes from D to F, totally skipping E. Would making an eBook put my work in ungraded limbo? E for effort, though, that's in the lexicon.

I don't say these things to Janet.

"An eBook's cheap. People buy them. You can have it converted into an app. My client wrote a self-help book about succeeding in the stock market. He turned it into an eBook and an app. Once you enter your portfolio, the app gives updated stock reports and net worth, buy and sell recommendations, research articles. He's a broker and knows the stock game. He gave his clients a coupon—buy the app, get the eBook. He makes almost as much money selling the app as he does as a broker."

"Really?"

"No. But I'm a marketer, it's what I'm supposed to say."

I realize now that she's
had enough to drink.

"Want some coffee? Or perhaps you'd
prefer a nightcap at my place?" I ask casually.

She looks at me. My nicks and
dents are probably out of focus.
She gives me a little smile.

Alice frowns at me as Janet and
I slip toward the door while she's
serving coffee. I smile back at her.

Sometimes, I'm like a cracked mirror
reflecting her own image back at Alice.
Usually, this is on her fifth or sixth drink.

There is a crack in everything, I
realize fleetingly, as Janet and I exit.

§

144

Final Destination

Sometimes hope died, often just outside
a church on the way to a funeral of some
family member he could barely recall.
What was her name, aunt somebody...
his name, cousin somebody else? Still,
outside the church on these occasions,
he realized that a funeral only served
to show that whoever it is had recently
arrived at the final destination of us all.

Now he knew the name, knew the
time of arrival at the destination, knew
how many hours had passed since.

His father looked out the window. "It's not supposed to be this way. My children should outlive me."

"We all end up in the same place," he answered. "Does it really matter so much when?"

"Yes. It matters to me. When, for my children, should be anytime after me."

His father's answer was relative, and that made sense to him somehow. This lonely feeling was also relative.

Still, "There are no guarantees, Dad, only that we arrive at the end."

"My children were supposed to mourn me, not the other way around."

Clichés, but what else was there to say?

"Well, I'll do my best to accommodate you, and wait until after you're gone."

His father turned and faced him.

"I'd appreciate that."

His brother's funeral stretched out through a church service, a graveside service, an afternoon of sympathetic visitors bringing food, and an evening of cousins, aunts, uncles who did not know each other that well staring across an over-burdened table.

The next morning, he woke up early and walked out into the backyard. His father already sat in one of the deck chairs arranged around a table, drinking coffee.

"The pot's on in the kitchen, if you want some."

After a pause where it was evident he wasn't going back into the kitchen, his father sighed.

"What next?"

"What do you mean?"

"Will we become a whole family again?"

"We did it after Mom died. We'll do it after this."

Hope kept shrinking, little by little. Unnamed and unremembered family members closed round, but could not fill the gaps left by a mother and a brother.

His father sipped his coffee. He put a hand on the old man's shoulder.

"I have to get back. I'm due on a flight to London tonight."

His father nodded.

"You know," he said, "there is one way."

"For what?"

"To make sure I don't have to arrange your funeral."

"Dad, it'll be ok. I'll be back in time to join you for the weekend."

His father nodded again.

"Goodbye, dad."

His father nodded, and sipped his coffee as his other son left. He decided to never get up from this chair.

He nodded again, one last time.

§

Words

Lately, the writer ~~deleted more than she typed. She'd write something, then bang, delete most of the remaining text. She left three words of thirty-six, just under ten-percent.~~

~~Those three remaining words weren't gold or silver pounded into jewelry by a hammer. They didn't excite her. They just weren't dead.~~

~~The thirty-three words she cut annoyed her, as school had. They didn't cohere. No living scene~~ emerged from them.

§

God's Pop Quiz

Humans? Two-legged dwellers of the
Earth? It's your Creator here. I know, I know,
it's been awhile since you've heard from
me. I've been busy up in the Oort Cloud.

I thought of coming down in a blaze
of Comet-ic glory, ride the fiery chariot
at the head of Ison. Then I thought, well,
maybe just step back to the front of the
class and get the lessons going again.

So, you've had time to study the
situation, no? You've been doing your
homework? A few of you have had
some, um, interesting projects. Anyway,
I think it's about time for a quiz.

Sh. Settle down. You had to know
something was coming. I mean, eventually
you knew it would come to this. I've got to
grade you somehow. If you've done your
homework, you should be well prepared.

Okay, pens and paper only on your desks.
C'mon. All phones and other electronic
devices, off. Put everything except your pen
and paper into your bags and your bags under
your chairs. Ready? You, back row, phone off
and tucked away in your bag. Now, please.

I'm going to give the questions
orally. The last time I wrote them
down, the tablets ended up in pieces
and we had to start all over again. I still
can't figure out why everyone went so
wild over a bit of metal statuary...

Let's see. Looks like everybody's ready. Here we go, first question:

1. Which is more important, your relationship with Me, an Ineffable and Unknown Being, or your relationship with your fellow humans, whom I also created? (Extra points for originality.)

Okay, you've all had enough time with that one. Next question.

2. If your Creator gave you a miraculous planet with water, land, resources for food, shelter and clothing, and all that you might need, should you:

a.) Use and abuse it at will without regard for care and upkeep.

b.) Grab all you can for yourself, friends, and relationships and keep the rest of Creation from touching any of it.

c.) Take it, process it, and sell it for vast profits.

d.) Consider it a gift and take care of it with an eye to sustaining the resources and planet into the future.

All you have to do is write the letter of your answer. It shouldn't take you ten pages to explain it.

3. If I, your Creator, am an Ineffable Being, and you, the Created, cannot possible know or understand me, explain religious dogma.

This one might take you ten pages or more to answer. I'll be back in a few generations to see how you're doing.

Acknowledgments

Earlier versions of pieces in this book appeared in *Bluzog* and *Meat for Tea: The Valley Review*. Both *The BeZine* and *The Woven Tale Press* included a number of pieces. Almost all of the writing in this book appeared on my blog (https://MichaelDickel. info), where you can still find the earlier versions, often with links and digital artwork included to further confuse you.

Almost all of the pieces in *The Toad's Garden* section and many in *The Palm Reader* section originated from experimental writing. Various prompts came from flash fiction sites, but the best experiments came from open invitations I posted on social media and on my blog for people to post five free-associated words for me to use. I would use them in groups for each new piece. Contributors, in alphabetical order include (apologies if I missed anyone): Stanley H. Barkan, Lucile Barker, Michele Baron, MaryLee Brag, Paulette Buche, Joanna Chen, Carolyn Hoople Creed, Cathy Crossan, Aviva (Frankel) Dekel (my loving wife), Jacqueline Dick, Rivkah Dickel (one of my amazing daughters), Paul Dickinson, Christine A. Farley. Jonathan Freed, Gabriella Garofalo, a blogger known as "godess of small things,", Jeffrey M. Green, Zena Hagerty, Lisa Holden, Chinedu Jonathan Ichu, Jerry Ingeman, Jonathan Jones, Ampat Koshy, Donna Kuhn, Elena (Zykova) Lacy, Kate Lamberg, gary lundy (my beloved fellow traveler in poetry and beyond), Aviva Luria, Mamta Madhavan, MaryAnn Franta Moenck, Alan Nettleton, Martina Reisz Newberry, Bozhidar Pangelov, Anna Patterson, Jen Pettit (one of my sisters-by-choice), Agnew T. Pickens, Lynn Pries, Nalini Priyadarshni, Louis Profeta, Donna Pryor-Foote, Julia Raymond (another of my amazing daughters), Steve Silberman (fellow photographer-hiker), Mike Stone (brother poet), Uwe W. Stroh, Susan Thornton, Jason Topp, Rayona Tuneelo, Monika Ashwin V (a strong supporter of my work), Peter Valentine, Michael Veloff, Steven Wadey, Eileen Walsh, Clare Washbrook, Nicholas Whittaker, Dane Zeller, and Verica Zivkovic. Some of these good people contributed more than once.

If you've read this far, and you think that you might like to contribute your own five words (please use free association to come up with them), visit my blog (https://MichaelDickel.info) and use the contact in the About section. You can contact me about other questions, comments, or appearances at the same place.

Ayelet Cohen directs, researches, and writes documentary films. She also creates silhouettes.

Michael Dickel co-edited *Voices Israel Volume 36* and was managing editor for *arc-23* and *arc-24*. His poetry books are *War Surrounds Us* (2015), *Midwest / Mid-East* (2012) and *The World Behind It, Chaos...* (2009).

MichaelDickel.info

www.ingramcontent.com/pod-product-compliance
Lightning Source LLC
Chambersburg PA
CBHW070034260626
47159CB00005B/2038